# Night and Morning, Volume 1

## Edward Bulwer Lytton

# Contents

PREFACE ...................................................................7

BOOK I. ....................................................................13
INTRODUCTORY CHAPTER. ....................................13
CHAPTER II. ..............................................................32
CHAPTER III. .............................................................39
CHAPTER IV. .............................................................43
CHAPTER V. ...............................................................56
CHAPTER VI. .............................................................66
CHAPTER VII. ............................................................90
CHAPTER VIII. ...........................................................93
CHAPTER IX. ............................................................110
CHAPTER X. .............................................................124
CHAPTER XI. ............................................................127

# NIGHT AND MORNING, VOLUME 1

BY

Edward Bulwer Lytton

# PREFACE

## TO THE EDITION OF 1845.

Much has been written by critics, especially by those in Germany (the native land of criticism), upon the important question, whether to please or to instruct should be the end of Fiction--whether a moral purpose is or is not in harmony with the undidactic spirit perceptible in the higher works of the imagination. And the general result of the discussion has been in favour of those who have contended that Moral Design, rigidly so called, should be excluded from the aims of the Poet; that his Art should regard only the Beautiful, and be contented with the indirect moral tendencies, which can never fail the creation of the Beautiful. Certainly, in fiction, to interest, to please, and sportively to elevate --to take man from the low passions, and the miserable troubles of life, into a higher region, to beguile weary and selfish pain, to excite a genuine sorrow at vicissitudes not his own, to raise the passions into sympathy with heroic struggles--and to admit the soul into that serener atmosphere from which it rarely returns to ordinary existence, without some memory or association which ought to enlarge the domain of thought and exalt the motives of action;--such, without other moral result or object, may satisfy the Poet,* and constitute the highest and most universal morality he can effect. But subordinate to this, which is not the duty, but the necessity, of all Fiction that outlasts the hour, the writer of imagination may well permit to himself other purposes and objects, taking care that they be not too sharply defined, and too obviously meant to contract the Poet into the Lecturer--the Fiction into the Homily. The delight in Shylock is not less vivid for the Humanity it latently but profoundly inculcates; the healthful merriment of the Tartufe is not less enjoyed for the exposure of the Hypocrisy it denounces. We need not demand from Shakespeare or from Moliere other morality than that which Genius unconsciously throws around it--the natural light which it reflects; but if some great principle which guides us practically in the daily intercourse with men becomes in the general lustre more clear and more pronounced, we gain doubly, by the general tendency and the particular result.

*[I use the word Poet in its proper sense, as applicable to any writer, whether in verse or prose, who invents or creates.]

Long since, in searching for new regions in the Art to which I am a servant, it seemed to me that they might be found lying far, and rarely trodden, beyond that range of conventional morality in which Novelist after Novelist had entrenched himself--amongst those subtle recesses in the ethics of human life in which Truth and Falsehood dwell undisturbed and unseparated. The vast and dark Poetry around us--the Poetry of Modern Civilisation and Daily Existence, is shut out from us in much, by the shadowy giants of Prejudice and Fear. He who would arrive at the Fairy Land must face the Phantoms. Betimes, I set myself to the task of investigating the motley world to which our progress in humanity--has attained, caring little what misrepresentation I incurred, what hostility I provoked, in searching through a devious labyrinth for the foot-tracks of Truth.

In the pursuit of this object, I am, not vainly, conscious that I have had my influence on my time--that I have contributed, though humbly and indirectly, to the benefits which Public Opinion has extorted from Governments and Laws. While (to content myself with a single example) the ignorant or malicious were decrying the moral of Paul Clifford, I consoled myself with perceiving that its truths had stricken deep--that many, whom formal essays might not reach, were enlisted by the picture and the popular force of Fiction into the service of that large and Catholic Humanity which frankly examines into the causes of crime, which ameliorates the ills of society by seeking to amend the circumstances by which they are occasioned; and commences the great work of justice to mankind by proportioning the punishment to the offence. That work, I know, had its share in the wise and great relaxation of our Criminal Code--it has had its share in results yet more valuable, because leading to more comprehensive reforms-viz., in the courageous facing of the ills which the mock decorum of timidity would shun to contemplate, but which, till fairly fronted, in the spirit of practical Christianity, sap daily, more and more, the walls in which blind Indolence would protect itself from restless Misery and rampant Hunger. For it is not till Art has told the unthinking that nothing (rightly treated) is too low for its breath to vivify and its wings to raise, that the Herd awaken from their chronic lethargy of contempt, and the Lawgiver is compelled to redress what the Poet has lifted into esteem. In thus enlarging the boundaries of the Novelist, from trite and conventional to untrodden ends, I have seen, not with the jealousy of an author, but with the pride of an Originator, that I have served as a guide to later and abler writers, both in England and abroad. If at times, while imitating, they have mistaken me, I am not. answerable for their errors; or if, more often, they have improved where they borrowed, I am not envious of their laurels. They owe me at least this, that I prepared the way for their reception, and that they would have been less popular and more misrepresented, if the outcry which bursts upon the first researches into new directions had not exhausted its noisy vehemence upon me.

In this Novel of **Night and Morning** I have had various ends in view-- subordinate, I grant, to the higher and more durable morality which belongs to the Ideal, and instructs us playfully while it interests, in the passions, and through the heart. First--to deal fearlessly with that universal unsoundness in social justice which makes distinctions so

marked and iniquitous between Vice and Crime--viz., between the
corrupting habits and the violent act--which scarce touches the former
with the lightest twig in the fasces--which lifts against the latter the
edge of the Lictor's axe.  Let a child steal an apple in sport, let a
starveling steal a roll in despair, and Law conducts them to the Prison,
for evil commune to mellow them for the gibbet.  But let a man spend one
apprenticeship from youth to old age in vice--let him devote a fortune,
perhaps colossal, to the wholesale demoralisation of his kind--and he may
be surrounded with the adulation of the so-called virtuous, and be served
upon its knee, by that Lackey--the Modern World!  I say not that Law can,
or that Law should, reach the Vice as it does the Crime; but I say, that
Opinion may be more than the servile shadow of Law.  I impress not here,
as in **Paul Clifford**, a material moral to work its effect on the
Journals, at the Hastings, through Constituents, and on Legislation;--I
direct myself to a channel less active, more tardy, but as sure--to the
Conscience--that reigns elder and superior to all Law, in men's hearts
and souls;--I utter boldly and loudly a truth, if not all untold,
murmured feebly and falteringly before, sooner or later it will find its
way into the judgment and the conduct, and shape out a tribunal which
requires not robe or ermine.

Secondly--In this work I have sought to lift the mask from the timid
selfishness which too often with us bears the name of Respectability.
Purposely avoiding all attraction that may savour of extravagance,
patiently subduing every tone and every hue to the aspect of those whom
we meet daily in our thoroughfares, I have shown in Robert Beaufort the
man of decorous phrase and bloodless action--the systematic self-server--
in whom the world forgive the lack of all that is generous, warm, and
noble, in order to respect the passive acquiescence in methodical
conventions and hollow forms.  And how common such men are with us in
this century, and how inviting and how necessary their delineation, may
be seen in this,--that the popular and pre-eminent Observer of the age in
which we live has since placed their prototype in vigorous colours upon

imperishable canvas.--[Need I say that I allude to the Pecksniff of Mr. Dickens?]

There is yet another object with which I have identified my tale. I trust that I am not insensible to such advantages as arise from the diffusion of education really sound, and knowledge really available;--for these, as the right of my countrymen, I have contended always. But of late years there has been danger that what ought to be an important truth may be perverted into a pestilent fallacy. Whether for rich or for poor, disappointment must ever await the endeavour to give knowledge without labour, and experience without trial. Cheap literature and popular treatises do not in themselves suffice to fit the nerves of man for the strife below, and lift his aspirations, in healthful confidence above. He who seeks to divorce toil from knowledge deprives knowledge of its most valuable property.--the strengthening of the mind by exercise. We learn what really braces and elevates us only in proportion to the effort it costs us. Nor is it in Books alone, nor in Books chiefly, that we are made conscious of our strength as Men; Life is the great Schoolmaster, Experience the mighty Volume. He who has made one stern sacrifice of self has acquired more than he will ever glean from the odds and ends of popular philosophy. And the man the least scholastic may be more robust in the power that is knowledge, and approach nearer to the Arch-Seraphim, than Bacon himself, if he cling fast to two simple maxims--"Be honest in temptation, and in Adversity believe in God." Such moral, attempted before in Eugene Aram, I have enforced more directly here; and out of such convictions I have created hero and heroine, placing them in their primitive and natural characters, with aid more from life than books,-- from courage the one, from affection the other--amidst the feeble Hermaphrodites of our sickly civilisation;--examples of resolute Manhood and tender Womanhood.

The opinions I have here put forth are not in fashion at this day. But I have never consulted the popular any more than the sectarian, Prejudice.

Alone and unaided I have hewn out my way, from first to last, by the force of my own convictions. The corn springs up in the field centuries after the first sower is forgotten. Works may perish with the workman; but, if truthful, their results are in the works of others, imitating, borrowing, enlarging, and improving, in the everlasting Cycle of Industry and Thought.

Knebworth, 1845.


# NOTE TO THE PRESENT EDITION, 1851.

I have nothing to add to the preceding pages, written six years ago, as to the objects and aims of this work; except to say, and by no means as a boast, that the work lays claims to one kind of interest which I certainly never desired to effect for it--viz., in exemplifying the glorious uncertainty of the Law. For, humbly aware of the blunders which Novelists not belonging to the legal profession are apt to commit, when they summon to the *denouement* of a plot the aid of a deity so mysterious as Themis, I submitted to an eminent lawyer the whole case of "Beaufort versus Beaufort," as it stands in this Novel. And the pages which refer to that suit were not only written from the opinion annexed to the brief I sent in, but submitted to the eye of my counsel, and revised by his pen.--(N.B. He was feed.) Judge then my dismay when I heard long afterwards that the late Mr. O'Connell disputed the soundness of the law I had thus bought and paid for! "Who shall decide when doctors disagree?" All I can say is, that I took the best opinion that love or money could get me; and I should add, that my lawyer, unawed by the alleged *ipse dixit* of the great Agitator (to be sure, he is dead), still stoutly maintains his own views of the question.

[I have, however, thought it prudent so far to meet the objection suggested by Mr. O'Connell, as to make a slight alteration in this edition, which will probably prevent the objection, if correct, being of any material practical effect on the disposition of that visionary El Dorado--the Beaufort Property.]

Let me hope that the right heir will live long enough to come under the Statute of Limitations.  Possession is nine points of the law, and Time may give the tenth.

Knebworth.

# NIGHT AND MORNING.

# BOOK I.

"Noch in meines Lebens Lenze
War ich and ich wandert' aus,
Und der Jugend frohe Tanze
Liess ich in des Vaters Haus."

SCHILLER, Der Pilgrim.

## INTRODUCTORY CHAPTER.

"Now rests our vicar.  They who knew him best,
Proclaim his life to have been entirely rest;
Not one so old has left this world of sin,

More like the being that he entered in."--CRABBE.

In one of the Welsh counties is a small village called A----. It is somewhat removed from the high road, and is, therefore, but little known to those luxurious amateurs of the picturesque, who view nature through the windows of a carriage and four. Nor, indeed, is there anything, whether of scenery or association, in the place itself, sufficient to allure the more sturdy enthusiast from the beaten tracks which tourists and guide-books prescribe to those who search the Sublime and Beautiful amidst the mountain homes of the ancient Britons. Still, on the whole, the village is not without its attractions. It is placed in a small valley, through which winds and leaps down many a rocky fall, a clear, babbling, noisy rivulet, that affords excellent sport to the brethren of the angle. Thither, accordingly, in the summer season occasionally resort the Waltons of the neighbourhood--young farmers, retired traders, with now and then a stray artist, or a roving student from one of the universities. Hence the solitary hostelry of A----, being somewhat more frequented, is also more clean and comfortable than could reasonably be anticipated from the insignificance and remoteness of the village.

At a time in which my narrative opens, the village boasted a sociable, agreeable, careless, half-starved parson, who never failed to introduce himself to any of the anglers who, during the summer months, passed a day or two in the little valley. The Rev. Mr. Caleb Price had been educated at the University of Cambridge, where he had contrived, in three years, to run through a little fortune of L3500. It is true, that he acquired in return the art of making milkpunch, the science of pugilism, and the reputation of one of the best-natured, rattling, open-hearted companions whom you could desire by your side in a tandem to Newmarket, or in a row with the bargemen. By the help of these gifts and accomplishments, he had not failed to find favour, while his money lasted, with the young aristocracy of the "Gentle Mother." And, though the very reverse of an ambitious or calculating man, he had certainly nourished the belief that some one of the "hats" or "tinsel gowns"--i.e., young lords or fellow-commoners, with whom he was on such excellent terms, and who supped with him so often, would do something for him in the way of a living. But it so happened that when Mr. Caleb Price had, with a little difficulty, scrambled through his degree, and found himself a Bachelor of Arts and at the end of his finances, his grand acquaintances parted from him to their various posts in the State Militant of Life. And, with the exception of one, joyous and reckless as himself, Mr. Caleb Price found that when Money makes itself wings it flies away with our friends. As poor Price had earned no academical distinction, so he could expect no advancement from his college; no fellowship; no tutorship leading hereafter to livings, stalls, and deaneries. Poverty began already to stare him in the face, when the only friend who, having shared his prosperity, remained true to his adverse fate,--a friend, fortunately for him, of high connections and brilliant prospects--succeeded in obtaining for him the humble living of A----. To this primitive spot the once jovial roisterer cheerfully retired--contrived to live contented upon an income somewhat less than he had formerly given to his groom--preached very short sermons to a very scanty and ignorant congregation, some of whom only understood Welsh--did good to the poor and sick in his own careless, slovenly way--and, uncheered or unvexed by wife and children, he rose in summer with the lark and in winter went to bed at nine precisely, to save coals and candles. For the rest, he was the most skilful angler in the whole county; and so willing to communicate the results of his experience as to the most taking colour of the flies, and the most favoured haunts of the trout--that he had given especial orders at the inn, that whenever any strange gentleman came to fish, Mr. Caleb Price should be immediately sent for. In this, to be sure, our worthy pastor had his usual recompense. First, if the stranger were tolerably liberal, Mr. Price was asked to dinner at the inn; and, secondly, if this failed, from the poverty or the churlishness of the obliged party, Mr. Price still had an opportunity to hear the last news--to talk about the Great World--in a word, to exchange ideas, and perhaps to get an old newspaper, or an odd number of a magazine.

Now, it so happened that one afternoon in October, when the periodical excursions of the anglers, becoming gradually rarer and more rare, had altogether ceased, Mr. Caleb Price was summoned from his parlour in which he had been employed in the fabrication of a net for his cabbages, by a little white-headed boy, who came to say there was a gentleman at the inn who wished immediately to see him--a strange gentleman, who had never been there before.

Mr. Price threw down his net, seized his hat, and, in less than five minutes, he was in the best room of the little inn.

The person there awaiting him was a man who, though plainly clad in a velveteen shooting-jacket, had an air and mien greatly above those common to the pedestrian visitors of A----. He was tall, and of one of those athletic forms in which vigour in youth is too often followed by corpulence in age. At this period, however, in the full prime of manhood--the ample chest and sinewy limbs, seen to full advantage in their simple and manly dress--could not fail to excite that popular admiration which is always given to strength in the one sex as to delicacy in the other. The stranger was walking impatiently to and fro the small apartment when Mr. Price entered; and then, turning to the clergyman a countenance handsome and striking, but yet more prepossessing from its expression of frankness than from the regularity of its features,--he stopped short, held out his hand, and said, with a gay laugh, as he glanced over the parson's threadbare and slovenly costume, "My poor Caleb!--what a metamorphosis!--I should not have known you again!"

"What! you! Is it possible, my dear fellow?--how glad I am to see you! What on earth can bring you to such a place? No! not a soul would believe me if I said I had seen you in this miserable hole."

"That is precisely the reason why I am here.  Sit down, Caleb, and we'll talk over matters as soon as our landlord has brought up the materials for--"

"The milk-punch," interrupted Mr. Price, rubbing his hands.

"Ah, that will bring us back to old times, indeed!"

In a few minutes the punch was prepared, and after two or three preparatory glasses, the stranger thus commenced: "My dear Caleb, I am in want of your assistance, and above all of your secrecy."

"I promise you both beforehand.  It will make me happy the rest of my life to think I have served my patron--my benefactor--the only friend I possess."

"Tush, man! don't talk of that: we shall do better for you one of these days.  But now to the point: I have come here to be married--married, old boy! married!"

And the stranger threw himself back in his chair, and chuckled with the glee of a schoolboy.

"Humph!" said the parson, gravely.  "It is a serious thing to do, and a very odd place to come to."

"I admit both propositions: this punch is superb.  To proceed.  You know that my uncle's immense fortune is at his own disposal; if I disobliged him, he would be capable of leaving all to my brother; I should disoblige him irrevocably if he knew that I had married a tradesman's daughter; I am going to marry a tradesman's daughter--a girl in a million! the ceremony must be as secret as possible.  And in this church, with you for the priest, I do not see a chance of discovery."

"Do you marry by license?"

"No, my intended is not of age; and we keep the secret even from her father.  In this village you will mumble over the bans without one of your congregation ever taking heed of the name.  I shall stay here a month for the purpose.  She is in London, on a visit to a relation in the city.  The bans on her side will be published with equal privacy in a little church near the Tower, where my name will be no less unknown than hers.  Oh, I've contrived it famously!"

"But, my dear fellow, consider what you risk."

"I have considered all, and I find every chance in my favour.  The bride will arrive here on the day of our wedding: my servant will be one witness; some stupid old Welshman, as antediluvian as possible--I leave it to you to select him--shall be the other.  My servant I shall dispose of, and the rest I can depend on."

"But--"

"I detest buts; if I had to make a language, I would not admit such a word in it.  And now, before I run on about Catherine, a subject quite inexhaustible, tell me, my dear friend, something about yourself."


    .     .     .     .     .     .     .


Somewhat more than a month had elapsed since the arrival of the stranger at the village inn.  He had changed his quarters for the Parsonage--went out but little, and then chiefly on foot excursions among the sequestered hills in the neighbourhood.  He was therefore but partially known by sight, even in the village; and the visit of some old college friend to the minister, though indeed it had never chanced before, was not, in itself, so remarkable an event as to excite any particular observation. The bans had been duly, and half audibly, hurried over, after the service was concluded, and while the scanty congregation were dispersing down the little aisle of the church,--when one morning a chaise and pair arrived at the Parsonage.  A servant out of livery leaped from the box.  The stranger opened the door of the chaise, and, uttering a joyous exclamation, gave his arm to a lady, who, trembling and agitated, could scarcely, even with that stalwart support, descend the steps.  "Ah!" she said, in a voice choked with tears, when they found themselves alone in the little parlour,--"ah! if you knew how I have suffered!"

How is it that certain words, and those the homeliest, which the hand writes and the eye reads as trite and commonplace expressions--when spoken convey so much,--so many meanings complicated and refined?  "Ah! if you knew how I have suffered!"

When the lover heard these words, his gay countenance fell; he drew back --his conscience smote him: in that complaint was the whole history of a clandestine love, not for both the parties, but for the woman--the painful secrecy--the remorseful deceit--the shame--the fear--the sacrifice.  She who uttered those words was scarcely sixteen.  It is an early age to leave Childhood behind for ever!

"My own love! you have suffered, indeed; but it is over now.

"Over!  And what will they say of me--what will they think of me at home? Over!  Ah!"

"It is but for a short time; in the course of nature my uncle cannot live long: all then will be explained.  Our marriage once made public, all connected with you will be proud to own you.  You will have wealth, station--a name among the first in the gentry of England.  But, above

all, you will have the happiness to think that your forbearance for a
time has saved me, and, it may be, our children, sweet one!--from poverty
and--"

"It is enough," interrupted the girl; and the expression of her
countenance became serene and elevated. "It is for you--for your sake.
I know what you hazard: how much I must owe you! Forgive me, this is the
last murmur you shall ever hear from these lips."

An hour after these words were spoken, the marriage ceremony was
concluded.

"Caleb," said the bridegroom, drawing the clergyman aside as they were
about to re-enter the house, "you will keep your promise, I know; and you
think I may depend implicitly upon the good faith of the witness you have
selected?"

"Upon his good faith?--no," said Caleb, smiling, "but upon his deafness,
his ignorance, and his age. My poor old clerk! He will have forgotten
all about it before this day three months. Now I have seen your lady, I
no longer wonder that you incur so great a risk. I never beheld so
lovely a countenance. You will be happy!" And the village priest
sighed, and thought of the coming winter and his own lonely hearth.

"My dear friend, you have only seen her beauty--it is her least charm.
Heaven knows how often I have made love; and this is the only woman I
have ever really loved. Caleb, there is an excellent living that adjoins
my uncle's house. The rector is old; when the house is mine, you will
not be long without the living. We shall be neighbours, Caleb, and then
you shall try and find a bride for yourself. Smith,"--and the bridegroom
turned to the servant who had accompanied his wife, and served as a
second witness to the marriage,--tell the post-boy to put to the horses
immediately."

"Yes, Sir.  May I speak a word with you?"

"Well, what?"

"Your uncle, sir, sent for me to come to him, the day before we left town."

"Aha!--indeed!"

"And I could just pick up among his servants that he had some suspicion-- at least, that he had been making inquiries--and seemed very cross, sir."

"You went to him?"

"No, Sir, I was afraid.  He has such a way with him;--whenever his eye is fixed on mine, I always feel as if it was impossible to tell a lie; and-- and--in short, I thought it was best not to go."

"You did right.  Confound this fellow!"  muttered the bridegroom, turning away; "he is honest, and loves me: yet, if my uncle sees him, he is clumsy enough to betray all.  Well, I always meant to get him out of the way--the sooner the better.  Smith!"

"Yes, sir!"

"You have often said that you should like, if you had some capital, to settle in Australia.  Your father is an excellent farmer; you are above the situation you hold with me; you are well educated, and have some knowledge of agriculture; you can scarcely fail to make a fortune as a settler; and if you are of the same mind still, why, look you, I have just L1000. at my bankers: you shall have half, if you like to sail by the first packet."

"Oh, sir, you are too generous."

"Nonsense--no thanks--I am more prudent than generous; for I agree with you that it is all up with me if my uncle gets hold of you. I dread my prying brother, too; in fact, the obligation is on my side; only stay abroad till I am a rich man, and my marriage made public, and then you may ask of me what you will. It's agreed, then; order the horses, we'll go round by Liverpool, and learn about the vessels. By the way, my good fellow, I hope you see nothing now of that good-for-nothing brother of yours?"

"No, indeed, sir. It's a thousand pities he has turned out so ill; for he was the cleverest of the family, and could always twist me round his little finger."

"That's the very reason I mentioned him. If he learned our secret, he would take it to an excellent market. Where is he?"

"Hiding, I suspect, sir."

"Well, we shall put the sea between you and him! So now all's safe."

Caleb stood by the porch of his house as the bride and bridegroom entered their humble vehicle. Though then November, the day was exquisitely mild and calm, the sky without a cloud, and even the leafless trees seemed to smile beneath the cheerful sun. And the young bride wept no more; she was with him she loved--she was his for ever. She forgot the rest. The hope--the heart of sixteen--spoke brightly out through the blushes that mantled over her fair cheeks. The bridegroom's frank and manly countenance was radiant with joy. As he waved his hand to Caleb from the window the post-boy cracked his whip, the servant settled himself on the dickey, the horses started off in a brisk trot,--the clergyman was left alone.

To be married is certainly an event in life; to marry other people is, for a priest, a very ordinary occurrence; and yet, from that day, a great change began to operate in the spirits and the habits of Caleb Price. Have you ever, my gentle reader, buried yourself for some time quietly in the lazy ease of a dull country-life? Have you ever become gradually accustomed to its monotony, and inured to its solitude; and, just at the time when you have half-forgotten the great world--that *mare magnum* that frets and roars in the distance--have you ever received in your calm retreat some visitor, full of the busy and excited life which you imagined yourself contented to relinquish? If so, have you not perceived, that, in proportion as his presence and communication either revived old memories, or brought before you new pictures of "the bright tumult" of that existence of which your guest made a part,--you began to compare him curiously with yourself; you began to feel that what before was to rest is now to rot; that your years are gliding from you unenjoyed and wasted; that the contrast between the animal life of passionate civilisation and the vegetable torpor of motionless seclusion is one that, if you are still young, it tasks your philosophy to bear,--feeling all the while that the torpor may be yours to your grave? And when your guest has left you, when you are again alone, is the solitude the same as it was before?

Our poor Caleb had for years rooted his thoughts to his village. His guest had been like the Bird in the Fairy Tale, settling upon the quiet branches, and singing so loudly and so gladly of the enchanted skies afar, that, when it flew away, the tree pined, nipped and withering in the sober sun in which before it had basked contented. The guest was, indeed, one of those men whose animal spirits exercise upon such as come within their circle the influence and power usually ascribed only to intellectual qualities. During the month he had sojourned with Caleb, he had brought back to the poor parson all the gaiety of the brisk and noisy novitiate that preceded the solemn vow and the dull retreat;--the social parties, the merry suppers, the open-handed, open-hearted fellowship of riotous, delightful, extravagant, thoughtless YOUTH. And Caleb was not a bookman--not a scholar; he had no resources in himself, no occupation but his indolent and ill-paid duties. The emotions, therefore, of the Active Man were easily aroused within him. But if this comparison between his past and present life rendered him restless and disturbed, how much more deeply and lastingly was he affected by a contrast between his own future and that of his friend! Not in those points where he could never hope equality--wealth and station--the conventional distinctions to which, after all, a man of ordinary sense must sooner or later reconcile himself--but in that one respect wherein all, high and low, pretend to the same rights--rights which a man of moderate warmth of feeling can never willingly renounce--viz., a partner in a lot however obscure; a kind face by a hearth, no matter how mean it be! And his happier friend, like all men full of life, was full of himself--full of his love, of his future, of the blessings of home, and wife, and children. Then, too, the young bride seemed so fair, so confiding, and so tender; so formed to grace the noblest or to cheer the humblest home! And both were so happy, so all in all to each other, as they left that barren threshold! And the priest felt all this, as, melancholy and envious, he turned from the door in that November day, to find himself thoroughly alone. He now began seriously to muse upon those fancied blessings which men wearied with celibacy see springing, heavenward, behind the altar. A few weeks afterwards a notable change was visible in the good man's exterior. He became more careful of his dress, he shaved every morning, he purchased a crop-eared Welsh cob; and it was soon known in the neighbourhood that the only journey the cob was ever condemned to take was to the house of a certain squire, who, amidst a family of all ages, boasted two very pretty marriageable daughters. That was the second holy day-time of poor Caleb --the love-romance of his life: it soon closed. On learning the amount of the pastor's stipend the squire refused to receive his addresses; and, shortly after, the girl to whom he had attached himself made what the

world calls a happy match: and perhaps it was one, for I never heard that
she regretted the forsaken lover.  Probably Caleb was not one of those
whose place in a woman's heart is never to be supplied.  The lady
married, the world went round as before, the brook danced as merrily
through the village, the poor worked on the week-days, and the urchins
gambolled round the gravestones on the Sabbath,--and the pastor's heart
was broken.  He languished gradually and silently away.  The villagers
observed that he had lost his old good-humoured smile; that he did not
stop every Saturday evening at the carrier's gate, to ask if there were
any news stirring in the town which the carrier weekly visited; that he
did not come to borrow the stray newspapers that now and then found their
way into the village; that, as he sauntered along the brookside, his
clothes hung loose on his limbs, and that he no longer "whistled as he
went;" alas, he was no longer "in want of thought!"  By degrees, the
walks themselves were suspended; the parson was no longer visible: a
stranger performed his duties.

One day, it might be some three years and more after the fatal visit I
have commemorated--one very wild rough day in early March, the postman,
who made the round of the district, rang at the parson's bell.  The
single female servant, her red hair loose on her neck, replied to the
call.

"And how is the master?"

"Very bad;" and the girl wiped her eyes.

"He should leave you something handsome," remarked the postman, kindly,
as he pocketed the money for the letter.

The pastor was in bed--the boisterous wind rattled clown the chimney and
shook the ill-fitting casement in its rotting frame.  The clothes he had
last worn were thrown carelessly about, unsmoothed, unbrushed; the scanty

articles of furniture were out of their proper places; slovenly discomfort marked the death-chamber.  And by the bedside stood a neighbouring clergyman, a stout, rustic, homely, thoroughly Welsh priest, who might have sat for the portrait of Parson Adams.

"Here's a letter for you," said the visitor.

"For me!" echoed Caleb, feebly.  "Ah--well--is it not very dark, or are my eyes failing?"  The clergyman and the servant drew aside the curtains and propped the sick man up: he read as follows, slowly, and with difficulty:

"DEAR, CALEB,--At last I can do something for you.  A friend of mine has a living in his gift just vacant, worth, I understand, from three to four hundred a year: pleasant neighbourhood--small parish.  And my friend keeps the hounds!--just the thing for you.  He is, however, a very particular sort of person--wants a companion, and has a horror of anything evangelical; wishes, therefore, to see you before he decides. If you can meet me in London, some day next month, I'll present you to him, and I have no doubt it will be settled.  You must think it strange I never wrote to you since we parted, but you know I never was a very good correspondent; and as I had nothing to communicate advantageous to you I thought it a sort of insult to enlarge on my own happiness, and so forth. All I shall say on that score is, that I've sown my wild oats; and that you may take my word for it, there's nothing that can make a man know how large, the heart is, and how little the world, till he comes home (perhaps after a hard day's hunting) and sees his own fireside, and hears one dear welcome; and--oh, by the way, Caleb, if you could but see my boy, the sturdiest little rogue!  But enough of this.  All that vexes me is, that I've never yet been able to declare my marriage: my uncle, however, suspects nothing: my wife bears up against all, like an angel as she is; still, in case of any accident, it occurs to me, now I'm writing to you, especially if you leave the place, that it may be as well to send

me an examined copy of the register.  In those remote places registers
are often lost or mislaid; and it may be useful hereafter, when I
proclaim the marriage, to clear up all doubt as to the fact.
"Good-bye, old fellow,
"Yours most truly, &c., &c."

"It comes too late," sighed Caleb, heavily; and the letter fell from his
hands.  There was a long pause.  "Close the shutters," said the sick man,
at last; "I think I could sleep: and--and--pick up that letter."

With a trembling, but eager gripe, he seized the paper, as a miser would
seize the deeds of an estate on which he has a mortgage.  He smoothed the
folds, looked complacently at the well-known hand, smiled--a ghastly
smile! and then placed the letter under his pillow, and sank down; they
left him alone.  He did not wake for some hours, and that good clergyman,
poor as himself, was again at his post.  The only friendships that are
really with us in the hour of need are those which are cemented by
equality of circumstance.  In the depth of home, in the hour of
tribulation, by the bed of death, the rich and the poor are seldom found
side by side.  Caleb was evidently much feebler; but his sense seemed
clearer than it had been, and the instincts of his native kindness were
the last that left him.  "There is something he wants me do for him," he
muttered.

"Ah! I remember: Jones, will you send for the parish register?  It is
somewhere in the vestry-room, I think--but nothing's kept properly.
Better go yourself--'tis important."

Mr. Jones nodded, and sallied forth.  The register was not in the vestry;
the church-wardens knew nothing about it; the clerk--a new clerk, who was
also the sexton, and rather a wild fellow--had gone ten miles off to a
wedding: every place was searched; till, at last, the book was found,

amidst a heap of old magazines and dusty papers, in the parlour of Caleb himself. By the time it was brought to him, the sufferer was fast declining; with some difficulty his dim eye discovered the place where, amidst the clumsy pothooks of the parishioners, the large clear hand of the old friend, and the trembling characters of the bride, looked forth, distinguished.

"Extract this for me, will you?" said Caleb. Mr. Jones obeyed.

"Now, just write above the extract:

"'Sir,--By Mr. Price's desire I send you the inclosed. He is too ill to write himself. But he bids me say that he has never been quite the same man since you left him; and that, if he should not get well again, still your kind letter has made him easier in his mind."

Caleb stopped.

"Go on."

"That is all I have to say: sign your name, and put the address--here it is. Ah, the letter," he muttered, "must not lie about! If anything happens to me, it may get him into trouble."

And as Mr. Jones sealed his communication, Caleb feebly stretched his wan hand, held the letter which had "come too late" over the flame of the candle. As the blazing paper dropped on the carpetless floor, Mr. Jones prudently set thereon the broad sole of his top-boot, and the maidservant brushed the tinder into the grate.

"Ah, trample it out:--hurry it amongst the ashes. The last as the rest," said Caleb, hoarsely. "Friendship, fortune, hope, love, life--a little flame, and then--and then--"

"Don't be uneasy--it's quite out!" said Mr. Jones. Caleb turned his face to the wall. He lingered till the next day, when he passed insensibly from sleep to death. As soon as the breath was out of his body, Mr. Jones felt that his duty was discharged, that other duties called him home. He promised to return to read the burial-service over the deceased, gave some hasty orders about the plain funeral, and was turning from the room, when he saw the letter he had written by Caleb's wish, still on the table. "I pass the post-office--I'll put it in," said he to the weeping servant; "and just give me that scrap of paper." So he wrote on the scrap, "P. S. He died this morning at half-past twelve, without pain.--M. J.;" and not taking the trouble to break the seal, thrust the final bulletin into the folds of the letter, which he then carefully placed in his vast pocket, and safely transferred to the post. And that was all that the jovial and happy man, to whom the letter was addressed, ever heard of the last days of his college friend.

The living, vacant by the death of Caleb Price, was not so valuable as to plague the patron with many applications. It continued vacant nearly the whole of the six months prescribed by law. And the desolate parsonage was committed to the charge of one of the villagers, who had occasionally assisted Caleb in the care of his little garden. The villager, his wife, and half-a-dozen noisy, ragged children, took possession of the quiet bachelor's abode. The furniture had been sold to pay the expenses of the funeral, and a few trifling bills; and, save the kitchen and the two attics, the empty house, uninhabited, was surrendered to the sportive mischief of the idle urchins, who prowled about the silent chambers in fear of the silence, and in ecstasy at the space. The bedroom in which Caleb had died was, indeed, long held sacred by infantine superstition. But one day the eldest boy having ventured across the threshold, two cupboards, the doors standing ajar, attracted the child's curiosity. He opened one, and his exclamation soon brought the rest of the children round him. Have you ever, reader, when a boy, suddenly stumbled on that

El Dorado, called by the grown-up folks a lumber room?  Lumber, indeed! what **Virtu** double-locks in cabinets is the real lumber to the boy! Lumber, reader! to thee it was a treasury!  Now this cupboard had been the lumber-room in Caleb's household.  In an instant the whole troop had thrown themselves on the motley contents.  Stray joints of clumsy fishing-rods; artificial baits; a pair of worn-out top-boots, in which one of the urchins, whooping and shouting, buried himself up to the middle; moth-eaten, stained, and ragged, the collegian's gown-relic of the dead man's palmy time; a bag of carpenter's tools, chiefly broken; a cricket-bat; an odd boxing-glove; a fencing-foil, snapped in the middle; and, more than all, some half-finished attempts at rude toys: a boat, a cart, a doll's house, in which the good-natured Caleb had busied himself for the younger ones of that family in which he had found the fatal ideal of his trite life.  One by one were these lugged forth from their dusty slumber-profane hands struggling for the first right of appropriation. And now, revealed against the wall, glared upon the startled violators of the sanctuary, with glassy eyes and horrent visage, a grim monster.  They huddled back one upon the other, pale and breathless, till the eldest, seeing that the creature moved not, took heart, approached on tip-toe-twice receded, and twice again advanced, and finally drew out, daubed, painted, and tricked forth in the semblance of a griffin, a gigantic kite.

The children, alas! were not old and wise enough to knew all the dormant value of that imprisoned aeronaut, which had cost Caleb many a dull evening's labour--the intended gift to the false one's favourite brother. But they guessed that it was a thing or spirit appertaining of right to them; and they resolved, after mature consultation, to impart the secret of their discovery to an old wooden-legged villager, who had served in the army, who was the idol of all the children of the place, and who, they firmly believed, knew everything under the sun, except the mystical arts of reading and writing.  Accordingly, having seen that the coast was clear--for they considered their parents (as the children of the hard-working often do) the natural foes to amusement--they carried the monster into an old outhouse, and ran to the veteran to beg him to come up slyly and inspect its properties.

Three months after this memorable event, arrived the new pastor--a slim, prim, orderly, and starch young man, framed by nature and trained by practice to bear a great deal of solitude and starving. Two loving couples had waited to be married till his Reverence should arrive. The ceremony performed, where was the registry-book? The vestry was searched-the church-wardens interrogated; the gay clerk, who, on the demise of his deaf predecessor, had come into office a little before Caleb's last illness, had a dim recollection of having taken the registry up to Mr. Price at the time the vestry-room was whitewashed. The house was searched-the cupboard, the, mysterious cupboard, was explored. "Here it is, sir!" cried the clerk; and he pounced upon a pale parchment volume. The thin clergyman opened it, and recoiled in dismay--more than three-fourths of the leaves had been torn out.

"It is the moths, sir," said the gardener's wife, who had not yet removed from the house.

The clergyman looked round; one of the children was trembling. "What have you done to this book, little one?"

"That book?--the--hi!--hi!--"

"Speak the truth, and you sha'n't be punished."

"I did not know it was any harm--hi!--hi!--"

"Well, and--"

"And old Ben helped us."

"Well?"

"And--and--and--hi!--hi!--The tail of the kite, sir!--"

"Where is the kite?"

Alas!  the kite and its tail were long ago gone to that undiscovered limbo where all things lost, broken, vanished, and destroyed; things that lose themselves--for servants are too honest to steal; things that break themselves--for servants are too careful to break; find an everlasting and impenetrable refuge.

"It does not signify a pin's head," said the clerk; "the parish must find a new 'un!"

"It is no fault of mine," said the Pastor.  "Are my chops ready?"

# CHAPTER II.

"And soothed with idle dreams the frowning fate."--CRABBE.

"Why does not my father come back?  what a time he has been away!"

"My dear Philip, business detains him; but he will be here in a few days --perhaps to-day!"

"I should like him to see how much I am improved."

"Improved in what, Philip?"  said the mother, with a smile.  "Not Latin,

I am sure; for I have not seen you open a book since you insisted on poor Todd's dismissal."

"Todd! Oh, he was such a scrub, and spoke through his nose: what could he know of Latin?"

"More than you ever will, I fear, unless--" and here there was a certain hesitation in the mother's voice, "unless your father consents to your going to school."

"Well, I should like to go to Eton! That's the only school for a gentleman. I've heard my father say so."

"Philip, you are too proud."--"Proud! you often call me proud; but, then, you kiss me when you do so. Kiss me now, mother."

The lady drew her son to her breast, put aside the clustering hair from his forehead, and kissed him; but the kiss was sad, and the moment after she pushed him away gently and muttered, unconscious that she was overheard:

"If, after all, my devotion to the father should wrong the children!"

The boy started, and a cloud passed over his brow; but he said nothing. A light step entered the room through the French casements that opened on the lawn, and the mother turned to her youngest-born, and her eye brightened.

"Mamma! mamma! here is a letter for you. I snatched it from John: it is papa's handwriting."

The lady uttered a joyous exclamation, and seized the letter. The younger child nestled himself on a stool at her feet, looking up while she read it; the elder stood apart, leaning on his gun, and with something of thought, even of gloom, upon his countenance.

There was a strong contrast in the two boys. The elder, who was about fifteen, seemed older than he was, not only from his height, but from the darkness of his complexion, and a certain proud, nay, imperious, expression upon features that, without having the soft and fluent graces of childhood, were yet regular and striking. His dark-green shooting-dress, with the belt and pouch, the cap, with its gold tassel set upon his luxuriant curls, which had the purple gloss of the raven's plume, blended perhaps something prematurely manly in his own tastes, with the love of the fantastic and the picturesque which bespeaks the presiding genius of the proud mother. The younger son had scarcely told his ninth year; and the soft, auburn ringlets, descending half-way down the shoulders; the rich and delicate bloom that exhibits at once the hardy health and the gentle fostering; the large deep-blue eyes; the flexile and almost effeminate contour of the harmonious features; altogether made such an ideal of childlike beauty as Lawrence had loved to paint or Chantrey model. And the daintiest cares of a mother, who, as yet, has her darling all to herself--her toy, her plaything--were visible in the large falling collar of finest cambric, and the blue velvet dress with its filigree buttons and embroidered sash.

Both the boys had about them the air of those whom Fate ushers blandly into life; the air of wealth, and birth, and luxury, spoiled and pampered as if earth had no thorn for their feet, and heaven not a wind to visit their young cheeks too roughly. The mother had been extremely handsome; and though the first bloom of youth was now gone, she had still the beauty that might captivate new love--an easier task than to retain the old. Both her sons, though differing from each other, resembled her; she had the features of the younger; and probably any one who had seen her in her own earlier youth would have recognized in that child's gay yet gentle countenance the mirror of the mother when a girl. Now, however,

especially when silent or thoughtful, the expression of her face was
rather that of the elder boy;--the cheek, once so rosy was now pale,
though clear, with something which time had given, of pride and thought,
in the curved lip and the high forehead.  One who could have looked on
her in her more lonely hours, might have seen that the pride had known
shame, and the thought was the shadow of the passions of fear and sorrow.

But now as she read those hasty, brief, but well-remembered characters--
read as one whose heart was in her eyes--joy and triumph alone were
visible in that eloquent countenance.  Her eyes flashed, her breast
heaved; and at length, clasping the letter to her lips, she kissed it
again and again with passionate transport.  Then, as her eyes met the
dark, inquiring, earnest gaze of her eldest born, she flung her arms
round him, and wept vehemently.

"What is the matter, mamma, dear mamma?" said the youngest, pushing
himself between Philip and his mother.  "Your father is coming back, this
day--this very hour;--and you--you--child--you, Philip--" Here sobs broke
in upon her words, and left her speechless.

The letter that had produced this effect ran as follows:

TO MRS MORTON, Fernside Cottage.

"DEAREST KATE,--My last letter prepared you for the news I have now to
relate--my poor uncle is no more.  Though I had seen little of him,
especially of late years, his death sensibly affected me; but I have at
least the consolation of thinking that there is nothing now to prevent my
doing justice to you.  I am the sole heir to his fortune--I have it in my
power, dearest Kate, to offer you a tardy recompense for all you have put
up with for my sake;--a sacred testimony to your long forbearance, your
unreproachful love, your wrongs, and your devotion.  Our children, too--
my noble Philip!--kiss them, Kate--kiss them for me a thousand times.

"I write in great haste--the burial is just over, and my letter will only serve to announce my return.  My darling Catherine, I shall be with you almost as soon as these lines meet your eyes--those clear eyes, that, for all the tears they have shed for my faults and follies, have never looked the less kind.  Yours, ever as ever,

"PHILIP BEAUFORT.

This letter has told its tale, and little remains to explain.  Philip Beaufort was one of those men of whom there are many in his peculiar class of society--easy, thoughtless, good-humoured, generous, with feelings infinitely better than his principles.

Inheriting himself but a moderate fortune, which was three parts in the hands of the Jews before he was twenty-five, he had the most brilliant expectations from his uncle; an old bachelor, who, from a courtier, had turned a misanthrope--cold--shrewd--penetrating--worldly--sarcastic--and imperious; and from this relation he received, meanwhile, a handsome and, indeed, munificent allowance.  About sixteen years before the date at which this narrative opens, Philip Beaufort had "run off," as the saying is, with Catherine Morton, then little more than a child,--a motherless child--educated at a boarding-school to notions and desires far beyond her station; for she was the daughter of a provincial tradesman.  And Philip Beaufort, in the prime of life, was possessed of most of the qualities that dazzle the eyes and many of the arts that betray the affections.  It was suspected by some that they were privately married: if so, the secret had been closely kept, and baffled all the inquiries of the stern old uncle.  Still there was much, not only in the manner, at once modest and dignified, but in the character of Catherine, which was proud and high-spirited, to give colour to the suspicion.  Beaufort, a man naturally careless of forms, paid her a marked and punctilious respect; and his attachment was evidently one not only of passion, but of confidence and esteem. Time developed in her mental qualities far superior to those of Beaufort, and for these she had ample leisure of cultivation. To the influence derived from her mind and person she added that of a frank, affectionate, and winning disposition; their children cemented the bond between them. Mr. Beaufort was passionately attached to field sports. He lived the greater part of the year with Catherine, at the beautiful cottage to which he had built hunting stables that were the admiration of the county; and though the cottage was near London, the pleasures of the metropolis seldom allured him for more than a few days-- generally but a few hours-at a time; and he--always hurried back with renewed relish to what he considered his home.

Whatever the connection between Catherine and himself (and of the true nature of that connection, the Introductory Chapter has made the reader more enlightened than the world), her influence had, at least, weaned from all excesses, and many follies, a man who, before he knew her, had seemed likely, from the extreme joviality and carelessness of his nature, and a very imperfect education, to contract whatever vices were most in fashion as preservatives against *ennui*. And if their union had been openly hallowed by the Church, Philip Beaufort had been universally esteemed the model of a tender husband and a fond father. Ever, as he became more and more acquainted with Catherine's natural good qualities, and more and more attached to his home, had Mr. Beaufort, with the generosity of true affection, desired to remove from her the pain of an equivocal condition by a public marriage. But Mr. Beaufort, though generous, was not free from the worldliness which had met him everywhere, amidst the society in which his youth had been spent. His uncle, the head of one of those families which yearly vanish from the commonalty into the peerage, but which once formed a distinguished peculiarity in the aristocracy of England--families of ancient birth, immense possessions, at once noble and untitled--held his estates by no other tenure than his own caprice. Though he professed to like Philip, yet he saw but little of him.  When the news of the illicit connection his nephew was reported to have formed reached him, he at first resolved to break it off; but observing that Philip no longer gambled, nor ran in debt, and had retired from the turf to the safer and more economical pastimes of the field, he contented himself with inquiries which satisfied him that Philip was not married; and perhaps he thought it, on the whole, more prudent to wink at an error that was not attended by the bills which had here-to-fore characterised the human infirmities of his reckless nephew.  He took care, however, incidentally, and in reference to some scandal of the day, to pronounce his opinion, not upon the fault, but upon the only mode of repairing it.

"If ever," said he, and he looked grimly at Philip while he spoke, "a gentleman were to disgrace his ancestry by introducing into his family one whom his own sister could not receive at her house, why, he ought to sink to her level, and wealth would but make his disgrace the more notorious.  If I had an only son, and that son were booby enough to do anything so discreditable as to marry beneath him, I would rather have my footman for my successor.  You understand, Phil!"

Philip did understand, and looked round at the noble house and the stately park, and his generosity was not equal to the trial.  Catherine --so great was her power over him--might, perhaps, have easily triumphed over his more selfish calculations; but her love was too delicate ever to breathe, of itself, the hope that lay deepest at her heart.  And her children!--ah! for them she pined, but for them she also hoped.  Before them was a long future, and she had all confidence in Philip.  Of late, there had been considerable doubts how far the elder Beaufort would realise the expectations in which his nephew had been reared.  Philip's younger brother had been much with the old gentleman, and appeared to be in high favour: this brother was a man in every respect the opposite to Philip--sober, supple, decorous, ambitious, with a face of smiles and a heart of ice.

But the old gentleman was taken dangerously ill, and Philip was summoned to his bed of death. Robert, the younger brother, was there also, with his wife (who he had married prudently) and his children (he had two, a son and a daughter). Not a word did the uncle say as to the disposition of his property till an hour before he died. And then, turning in his bed, he looked first at one nephew, then at the other, and faltered out:

"Philip, you are a scapegrace, but a gentleman! Robert, you are a careful, sober, plausible man; and it is a great pity you were not in business; you would have made a fortune!--you won't inherit one, though you think it: I have marked you, sir. Philip, beware of your brother. Now let me see the parson."

The old man died; the will was read; and Philip succeeded to a rental of L20,000. a-year; Robert, to a diamond ring, a gold repeater, L5,000. and a curious collection of bottled snakes.

# CHAPTER III.

"Stay, delightful Dream;

Let him within his pleasant garden walk;
Give him her arm--of blessings let them talk."--CRABBE.

"There, Robert, there! now you can see the new stables. By Jove, they are the completest thing in the three kingdoms!"

"Quite a pile! But is that the house? You lodge your horses more magnificently than yourself."

"But is it not a beautiful cottage?--to be sure, it owes everything to Catherine's taste. Dear Catherine!"

Mr. Robert Beaufort, for this colloquy took place between the brothers, as their britska rapidly descended the hill, at the foot of which lay Fernside Cottage and its miniature demesnes--Mr. Robert Beaufort pulled his travelling cap over his brows, and his countenance fell, whether at the name of Catherine, or the tone in which the name was uttered; and there was a pause, broken by a third occupant of the britska, a youth of about seventeen, who sat opposite the brothers.

"And who are those boys on the lawn, uncle?"

"Who are those boys?" It was a simple question, but it grated on the ear of Mr. Robert Beaufort--it struck discord at his heart. "Who were those boys?" as they ran across the sward, eager to welcome their father home; the westering sun shining full on their joyous faces--their young forms so lithe and so graceful--their merry laughter ringing in the still air. "Those boys," thought Mr. Robert Beaufort, "the sons of shame, rob mine of his inheritance." The elder brother turned round at his nephew's question, and saw the expression on Robert's face. He bit his lip, and answered, gravely:

"Arthur, they are my children."

"I did not know you were married," replied Arthur, bending forward to take a better view of his cousins.

Mr. Robert Beaufort smiled bitterly, and Philip's brow grew crimson.

The carriage stopped at the little lodge. Philip opened the door, and jumped to the ground; the brother and his son followed. A moment more, and Philip was locked in Catherine's arms, her tears falling fast upon his breast; his children plucking at his coat; and the younger one crying in his shrill, impatient treble, "Papa! papa! you don't see Sidney, papa!"

Mr. Robert Beaufort placed his hand on his son's shoulder, and arrested his steps, as they contemplated the group before them.

"Arthur," said he, in a hollow whisper, "those children are our disgrace and your supplanters; they are bastards! bastards! and they are to be his heirs!"

Arthur made no answer, but the smile with which be had hitherto gazed on his new relations vanished.

"Kate," said Mr. Beaufort, as he turned from Mrs. Morton, and lifted his youngest-born in his arms, "this is my brother and his son: they are welcome, are they not?"

Mr. Robert bowed low, and extended his hand, with stiff affability, to Mrs. Morton, muttering something equally complimentary and inaudible.

The party proceeded towards the house. Philip and Arthur brought up the rear.

"Do you shoot?" asked Arthur, observing the gun in his cousin's hand.

"Yes. I hope this season to bag as many head as my father: he is a famous shot. But this is only a single barrel, and an old-fashioned sort of detonator. My father must get me one of the new gulls. I can't afford it myself."

"I should think not," said Arthur, smiling.

"Oh, as to that," resumed Philip, quickly, and with a heightened colour, "I could have managed it very well if I had not given thirty guineas for a brace of pointers the other day: they are the best dogs you ever saw."

"Thirty guineas!" echoed Arthur, looking with native surprise at the speaker; "why, how old are you?"

"Just fifteen last birthday. Holla, John! John Green!" cried the young gentleman in an imperious voice, to one of the gardeners, who was crossing the lawn, "see that the nets are taken down to the lake to-morrow, and that my tent is pitched properly, by the lime-trees, by nine o'clock. I hope you will understand me this time: Heaven knows you take a deal of telling before you understand anything!"

"Yes, Mr. Philip," said the man, bowing obsequiously; and then muttered, as he went off, "Drat the nat'rel! He speaks to a poor man as if he warn't flesh and blood."

"Does your father keep hunters?" asked Philip. No."

"Why?"

"Perhaps one reason may be, that he is not rich enough."

"Oh! that's a pity. Never mind, we'll mount you, whenever you like to pay us a visit."

Young Arthur drew himself up, and his air, naturally frank and gentle, became haughty and reserved. Philip gazed on him, and felt offended; he scarce knew why, but from that moment he conceived a dislike to his cousin.

# CHAPTER IV.

"For a man is helpless and vain, of a condition so exposed to calamity that a raisin is able to kill him; any trooper out of the Egyptian army--a fly can do it, when it goes on God's errand."--JEREMY TAYLOR *On the Deceitfulness of the Heart*.

The two brothers sat at their wine after dinner.  Robert sipped claret, the sturdy Philip quaffed his more generous port.  Catherine and the boys might be seen at a little distance, and by the light of a soft August moon, among the shrubs and boseluets of the lawn.

Philip Beaufort was about five-and-forty, tall, robust, nay, of great strength of frame and limb; with a countenance extremely winning, not only from the comeliness of its features, but its frankness, manliness, and good nature.  His was the bronzed, rich complexion, the inclination towards embonpoint, the athletic girth of chest, which denote redundant health, and mirthful temper, and sanguine blood.  Robert, who had lived the life of cities, was a year younger than his brother; nearly as tall, but pale, meagre, stooping, and with a careworn, anxious, hungry look, which made the smile that hung upon his lips seem hollow and artificial.  His dress, though plain, was neat and studied; his manner, bland and plausible; his voice, sweet and low: there was that about him which, if it did not win liking, tended to excite respect--a certain decorum, a nameless propriety of appearance and bearing, that approached a little to formality: his every movement, slow and measured, was that of one who paced in the circle that fences round the habits and usages of the world.

"Yes," said Philip, "I had always decided to take this step, whenever my poor uncle's death should allow me to do so.  You have seen Catherine, but you do not know half her good qualities: she would grace any station; and, besides, she nursed me so carefully last year, when I broke my collar-bone in that cursed steeple-chase. Egad, I am getting too heavy and growing too old for such schoolboy pranks."

"I have no doubt of Mrs. Morton's excellence, and I honour your motives; still, when you talk of her gracing any station, you must not forget, my dear brother, that she will be no more received as Mrs. Beaufort than she is now as Mrs. Morton."

"But I tell you, Robert, that I am really married to her already; that she would never have left her home but on that condition; that we were married the very day we met after her flight."

Robert's thin lips broke into a slight sneer of incredulity. "My dear brother, you do right to say this--any man in your situation would say the same. But I know that my uncle took every pains to ascertain if the report of a private marriage were true."

"And you helped him in the search. Eh, Bob?"

Bob slightly blushed. Philip went on.

"Ha, ha! to be sure you did; you knew that such a discovery would have done for me in the old gentleman's good opinion. But I blinded you both, ha, ha! The fact is, that we were married with the greatest privacy; that even now, I own, it would be difficult for Catherine herself to establish the fact, unless I wished it. I am ashamed to think that I have never even told her where I keep the main proof of the marriage. I induced one witness to leave the country, the other must be long since dead: my poor friend, too, who officiated, is no more. Even the register, Bob, the register itself, has been destroyed: and yet, notwithstanding, I will prove the ceremony and clear up poor Catherine's fame; for I have the attested copy of the register safe and sound. Catherine not married! why, look at her, man!"

Mr. Robert Beaufort glanced at the window for a moment, but his countenance was still that of one unconvinced. "Well, brother," said he, dipping his fingers in the water-glass, "it is not for me to contradict you. It is a very curious tale--parson dead--witnesses missing. But still, as I said before, if you are resolved on a public marriage, you are wise to insist that there has been a previous private one. Yet, believe me, Philip," continued Robert, with solemn earnestness, "the world--"

"Damn the world! What do I care for the world! We don't want to go to routs and balls, and give dinners to fine people. I shall live much the same as I have always done; only, I shall now keep the hounds--they are very indifferently kept at present--and have a yacht; and engage the best masters for the boys. Phil wants to go to Eton, but I know what Eton is: poor fellow! his feelings might be hurt there, if others are as sceptical as yourself. I suppose my old friends will not be less civil now I have L20,000. a year. And as for the society of women, between you and me, I don't care a rush for any woman but Catherine: poor Katty!"

"Well, you are the best judge of your own affairs: you don't misinterpret my motives?"

"My dear Bob, no. I am quite sensible how kind it is in you--a man of your starch habits and strict views, coming here to pay a mark of respect to Kate (Mr. Robert turned uneasily in his chair)--even before you knew of the private marriage, and I'm sure I don't blame you for never having done it before. You did quite right to try your chance with my uncle."

Mr. Robert turned in his chair again, still more uneasily, and cleared his voice as if to speak. But Philip tossed off his wine, and proceeded, without heeding his brother,--

"And though the poor old man does not seem to have liked you the better for consulting his scruples, yet we must make up for the partiality of his will.  Let me see--what with your wife's fortune, you muster L2000. a year?"

"Only L1500., Philip, and Arthur's education is growing expensive.  Next year he goes to college.  He is certainly very clever, and I have great hopes--"

"That he will do Honour to us all--so have I.  He is a noble young fellow: and I think my Philip may find a great deal to learn from him,-- Phil is a sad idle dog; but with a devil of a spirit, and sharp as a needle.  I wish you could see him ride.  Well, to return to Arthur. Don't trouble yourself about his education--that shall be my care.  He shall go to Christ Church--a gentleman-commoner, of course--and when he is of age we'll get him into parliament.  Now for yourself, Bob.  I shall sell the town-house in Berkeley Square, and whatever it brings you shall have.  Besides that, I'll add L1500. a year to your L1000.--so that's said and done.  Pshaw! brothers should be brothers.--Let's come out and play with the boys!"

The two Beauforts stepped through the open casement into the lawn.

"You look pale, Bob--all you London fellows do.  As for me, I feel as strong as a horse: much better than when I was one of your gay dogs straying loose about the town'.  'Gad, I have never had a moment's ill health, except from a fall now and then.  I feel as if I should live for ever, and that's the reason why I could never make a will."

"Have you never, then, made your will?"

"Never as yet.  Faith, till now, I had little enough to leave.  But now that all this great Beaufort property is at my own disposal, I must think

of Kate's jointure. By Jove! now I speak of it, I will ride to ----
to-morrow, and consult the lawyer there both about the will and the
marriage. You will stay for the wedding?"

"Why, I must go into --shire to-morrow evening, to place Arthur with his
tutor. But I'll return for the wedding, if you particularly wish it:
only Mrs. Beaufort is a woman of very strict--"

"I--do particularly wish it," interrupted Philip, gravely; "for I desire,
for Catherine's sake, that you, my sole surviving relation, may not seem
to withhold your countenance from an act of justice to her. And as for
your wife, I fancy L1500. a year would reconcile her to my marrying out
of the Penitentiary."

Mr. Robert bowed his head, coughed huskily, and said, "I appreciate your
generous affection, Philip."

The next morning, while the elder parties were still over the breakfast-
table, the younger people were in the grounds it was a lovely day, one of
the last of the luxuriant August--and Arthur, as he looked round, thought
he had never seen a more beautiful place. It was, indeed, just the spot
to captivate a youthful and susceptible fancy. The village of Fernside,
though in one of the counties adjoining Middlesex, and as near to London
as the owner's passionate pursuits of the field would permit, was yet as
rural and sequestered as if a hundred miles distant from the smoke of the
huge city. Though the dwelling was called a cottage, Philip had enlarged
the original modest building into a villa of some pretensions. On either
side a graceful and well-proportioned portico stretched verandahs,
covered with roses and clematis; to the right extended a range of costly
conservatories, terminating in vistas of trellis-work which formed those
elegant alleys called rosaries, and served to screen the more useful
gardens from view. The lawn, smooth and even, was studded with American
plants and shrubs in flower, and bounded on one side by a small lake, on

the opposite bank of which limes and cedars threw their shadows over the clear waves. On the other side a light fence separated the grounds from a large paddock, in which three or four hunters grazed in indolent enjoyment. It was one of those cottages which bespeak the ease and luxury not often found in more ostentatious mansions--an abode which, at sixteen, the visitor contemplates with vague notions of poetry and love--which, at forty, he might think dull and d---d expensive-which, at sixty, he would pronounce to be damp in winter, and full of earwigs in the summer. Master Philip was leaning on his gun; Master Sidney was chasing a peacock butterfly; Arthur was silently gazing on the shining lake and the still foliage that drooped over its surface. In the countenance of this young man there was something that excited a certain interest. He was less handsome than Philip, but the expression of his face was more prepossessing. There was something of pride in the forehead; but of good nature, not unmixed with irresolution and weakness, in the curves of the mouth. He was more delicate of frame than Philip; and the colour of his complexion was not that of a robust constitution. His movements were graceful and self-possessed, and he had his father's sweetness of voice. "This is really beautiful!--I envy you, cousin Philip."

"Has not your father got a country-house?"

"No: we live either in London or at some hot, crowded watering-place."

"Yes; this is very nice during the shooting and hunting season. But my old nurse says we shall have a much finer place now. I liked this very well till I saw Lord Belville's place. But it is very unpleasant not to have the finest house in the county: *aut Caesar aut nullus*--that's my motto. Ah! do you see that swallow? I'll bet you a guinea I hit it." "No, poor thing! don't hurt it." But ere the remonstrance was uttered, the bird lay quivering on the ground. "It is just September, and one must keep one's hand in," said Philip, as he reloaded his gun.

To Arthur this action seemed a wanton cruelty; it was rather the wanton
recklessness which belongs to a wild boy accustomed to gratify the
impulse of the moment--the recklessness which is not cruelty in the boy,
but which prosperity may pamper into cruelty in the man. And scarce had
he reloaded his gun before the neigh of a young colt came from the
neighbouring paddock, and Philip bounded to the fence. "He calls me,
poor fellow; you shall see him feed from my hand. Run in for a piece of
bread--a large piece, Sidney." The boy and the animal seemed to
understand each other. "I see you don't like horses," he said to Arthur.
As for me, I love dogs, horses--every dumb creature."

"Except swallows." said Arthur, with a half smile, and a little
surprised at the inconsistency of the boast.

"Oh! that is short,--all fair: it is not to hurt the swallow--it is to
obtain skill," said Philip, colouring; and then, as if not quite easy
with his own definition, he turned away abruptly.

"This is dull work--suppose we fish. By Jove!" (he had caught his
father's expletive) "that blockhead has put the tent on the wrong side of
the lake, after all. Holla, you, sir!" and the unhappy gardener looked
up from his flower-beds; "what ails you? I have a great mind to tell my
father of you--you grow stupider every day. I told you to put the tent
under the lime-trees."

"We could not manage it, sir; the boughs were in the way."

"And why did you not cut the boughs, blockhead?"

"I did not dare do so, sir, without master's orders," said the man
doggedly.

"My orders are sufficient, I should think; so none of your impertinence," cried Philip, with a raised colour; and lifting his hand, in which he held his ramrod, he shook it menacingly over the gardener's head,--"I've a great mind to----"

"What's the matter, Philip?" cried the good-humoured voice of his father. "Fie!"

"This fellow does not mind what I say, sir."

"I did not like to cut the boughs of the lime-trees without your orders, sir," said the gardener.

"No, it would be a pity to cut them. You should consult me there, Master Philip;" and the father shook him by the collar with a good-natured, and affectionate, but rough sort of caress.

"Be quiet, father!" said the boy, petulantly and proudly; "or," he added, in a lower voice, but one which showed emotion, "my cousin may think you mean less kindly than you always do, sir."

The father was touched: "Go and cut the lime-boughs, John; and always do as Mr. Philip tells you."

The mother was behind, and she sighed audibly. "Ah! dearest, I fear you will spoil him."

"Is he not your son? and do we not owe him the more respect for having hitherto allowed others to--"

He stopped, and the mother could say no more. And thus it was, that this boy of powerful character and strong passions had, from motives the most amiable, been pampered from the darling into the despot.

"And now, Kate, I will, as I told you last night, ride over to ---- and fix the earliest day for our public marriage: I will ask the lawyer to dine here, to talk about the proper steps for proving the private one."

"Will that be difficult" asked Catherine, with natural anxiety.

"No,--for if you remember, I had the precaution to get an examined copy of the register; otherwise, I own to you, I should have been alarmed. I don't know what has be come of Smith. I heard some time since from his father that he had left the colony; and (I never told you before--it would have made you uneasy) once, a few years ago, when my uncle again got it into his head that we might be married, I was afraid poor Caleb's successor might, by chance, betray us. So I went over to A---- myself, being near it when I was staying with Lord C----, in order to see how far it might be necessary to secure the parson; and, only think! I found an accident had happened to the register--so, as the clergyman could know nothing, I kept my own counsel. How lucky I have the copy! No doubt the lawyer will set all to rights; and, while I am making the settlements, I may as well make my will. I have plenty for both boys, but the dark one must be the heir. Does he not look born to be an eldest son?"

"Ah, Philip!"

"Pshaw! one don't die the sooner for making a will. Have I the air of a man in a consumption?"--and the sturdy sportsman glanced complacently at the strength and symmetry of his manly limbs. "Come, Phil, let's go to the stables. Now, Robert, I will show you what is better worth seeing than those miserable flower-beds." So saying, Mr. Beaufort led the way to the courtyard at the back of the cottage. Catherine and Sidney remained on the lawn; the rest followed the host. The grooms, of whom Beaufort was the idol, hastened to show how well the horses had thriven in his absence.

"Do see how Brown Bess has come on, sir! but, to be sure, Master Philip keeps her in exercise. Ah, sir, he will be as good a rider as your honour, one of these days."

"He ought to be a better, Tom; for I think he'll never have my weight to carry. Well, saddle Brown Bess for Mr. Philip. What horse shall I take? Ah! here's my old friend, Puppet!"

"I don't know what's come to Puppet, sir; he's off his feed, and turned sulky. I tried him over the bar yesterday; but he was quite restive like."

"The devil he was! So, so, old boy, you shall go over the six-barred gate to-day, or we'll know why." And Mr. Beaufort patted the sleek neck of his favourite hunter. "Put the saddle on him, Tom."

"Yes, your honour. I sometimes think he is hurt in the loins somehow--he don't take to his leaps kindly, and he always tries to bite when we bridles him. Be quiet, sir!"

"Only his airs," said Philip. I did not know this, or I would have taken him over the gate. Why did not you tell me, Tom?"

"Lord love you, sir! because you have such a spurret; and if anything had come to you--"

"Quite right: you are not weight enough for Puppet, my boy; and he never did like any one to back him but myself. What say you, brother, will you ride with us?"

"No, I must go to ---- to-day with Arthur. I have engaged the post-horses at two o'clock; but I shall be with you to-morrow or the day after. You see his tutor expects him; and as he is backward in his mathematics, he has no time to lose."

"Well, then, good-bye, nephew!" and Beaufort slipped a pocket-book into the boy's hand. "Tush! whenever you want money, don't trouble your father--write to me--we shall be always glad to see you; and you must teach Philip to like his book a little better--eh, Phil?"

"No, father; I shall be rich enough to do without books," said Philip, rather coarsely; but then observing the heightened colour of his cousin, he went up to him, and with a generous impulse said, "Arthur, you admired this gun; pray accept it. Nay, don't be shy--I can have as many as I like for the asking: you're not so well off, you know."

The intention was kind, but the manner was so patronising that Arthur felt offended. He put back the gun, and said, drily, "I shall have no occasion for the gun, thank you."

If Arthur was offended by the offer, Philip was much more offended by the refusal. "As you like; I hate pride," said he; and he gave the gun to the groom as he vaulted into his saddle with the lightness of a young Mercury. "Come, father!"

Mr. Beaufort had now mounted his favourite hunter--a large, powerful horse well known for its prowess in the field. The rider trotted him once or twice through the spacious yard.

"Nonsense, Tom: no more hurt in the loins than I am. Open that gate; we will go across the paddock, and take the gate yonder--the old six-bar-- eh, Phil?"

"Capital!--to be sure!--"

The gate was opened--the grooms stood watchful to see the leap, and a kindred curiosity arrested Robert Beaufort and his son.

How well they looked! those two horsemen; the ease, lightness, spirit of the one, with the fine-limbed and fiery steed that literally "bounded beneath him as a barb"--seemingly as gay, as ardent, and as haughty as the boyrider. And the manly, and almost herculean form of the elder Beaufort, which, from the buoyancy of its movements, and the supple grace that belongs to the perfect mastership of any athletic art, possessed an elegance and dignity, especially on horseback, which rarely accompanies proportions equally sturdy and robust. There was indeed something knightly and chivalrous in the bearing of the elder Beaufort--in his handsome aquiline features, the erectness of his mien, the very wave of his hand, as he spurred from the yard.

"What a fine-looking fellow my uncle is!" said Arthur, with involuntary admiration.

"Ay, an excellent life--amazingly strong!" returned the pale father, with a slight sigh.

"Philip," said Mr. Beaufort, as they cantered across the paddock, "I think the gate is too much for you. I will just take Puppet over, and then we will open it for you."

"Pooh, my dear father! you don't know how I'm improved!" And slackening the rein, and touching the side of his horse, the young rider darted forward and cleared the gate, which was of no common height, with an ease that extorted a loud "bravo" from the proud father.

"Now, Puppet," said Mr. Beaufort, spurring his own horse. The animal cantered towards the gate, and then suddenly turned round with an impatient and angry snort. "For shame, Puppet!--for shame, old boy!" said the sportsman, wheeling him again to the barrier. The horse shook

his head, as if in remonstrance; but the spur vigorously applied showed
him that his master would not listen to his mute reasonings. He bounded
forward--made at the gate--struck his hoofs against the top bar--fell
forward, and threw his rider head foremost on the road beyond. The horse
rose instantly--not so the master. The son dismounted, alarmed and
terrified. His father was speechless! and blood gushed from the mouth
and nostrils, as the head drooped heavily on the boy's breast. The
bystanders had witnessed the fall--they crowded to the spot--they took
the fallen man from the weak arms of the son--the head groom examined him
with the eye of one who had picked up science from his experience in such
casualties.

"Speak, brother!--where are you hurt?" exclaimed Robert Beaufort.

"He will never speak more!" said the groom, bursting into tears. "His
neck is broken!"

"Send for the nearest surgeon," cried Mr. Robert. "Good God! boy!
don't mount that devilish horse!"

But Arthur had already leaped on the unhappy steed, which had been the
cause of this appalling affliction. "Which way?"

"Straight on to ----, only two miles--every one knows Mr. Powis's house.
God bless you!" said the groom. Arthur vanished.

"Lift him carefully, and take him to the house," said Mr. Robert. "My
poor brother! my dear brother!"

He was interrupted by a cry, a single shrill, heartbreaking cry; and
Philip fell senseless to the ground.

No one heeded him at that hour--no one heeded the fatherless BASTARD.

"Gently, gently," said Mr. Robert, as he followed the servants and their load. And he then muttered to himself, and his sallow cheek grew bright, and his breath came short: "He has made no will--he never made a will."

# CHAPTER V.

"Constance. O boy, then where art thou?
*        * * * What becomes of me"--*King John*.

It was three days after the death of Philip Beaufort--for the surgeon arrived only to confirm the judgment of the groom: in the drawing-room of the cottage, the windows closed, lay the body, in its coffin, the lid not yet nailed down. There, prostrate on the floor, tearless, speechless, was the miserable Catherine; poor Sidney, too young to comprehend all his loss, sobbing at her side; while Philip apart, seated beside the coffin, gazed abstractedly on that cold rigid face which had never known one frown for his boyish follies.

In another room, that had been appropriated to the late owner, called his study, sat Robert Beaufort. Everything in this room spoke of the deceased. Partially separated from the rest of the house, it communicated by a winding staircase with a chamber above, to which Philip had been wont to betake himself whenever he returned late, and over-exhilarated, from some rural feast crowning a hard day's hunt. Above a quaint, old-fashioned bureau of Dutch workmanship (which Philip had picked up at a sale in the earlier years of his marriage) was a portrait of Catherine taken in the bloom of her youth. On a peg on the door that led to the staircase, still hung his rough driving coat. The window commanded the view of the paddock in which the worn-out hunter or the unbroken colt grazed at will. Around the walls of the "study"-- (a strange misnomer!)--hung prints of celebrated fox-hunts and renowned steeple-chases: guns, fishing-rods, and foxes' brushes, ranged with a sportsman's neatness, supplied the place of books.  On the mantelpiece lay a cigar-case, a well-worn volume on the Veterinary Art, and the last number of the Sporting Magazine.  And in the room--thus witnessing of the hardy, masculine, rural life, that had passed away--sallow, stooping, town-worn, sat, I say, Robert Beaufort, the heir-at-law,--alone: for the very day of the death he had remanded his son home with the letter that announced to his wife the change in their fortunes, and directed her to send his lawyer post-haste to the house of death.  The bureau, and the drawers, and the boxes which contained the papers of the deceased were open; their contents had been ransacked; no certificate of the private marriage, no hint of such an event; not a paper found to signify the last wishes of the rich dead man.

He had died, and made no sign.  Mr. Robert Beaufort's countenance was still and composed.

A knock at the door was heard; the lawyer entered.

"Sir, the undertakers are here, and Mr. Greaves has ordered the bells to be rung: at three o'clock he will read the service."

"I am obliged to you., Blackwell, for taking these melancholy offices on yourself.  My poor brother!--it is so sudden!  But the funeral, you say, ought to take place to-day?"

"The weather is so warm," said the lawyer, wiping his forehead.  As he spoke, the death-bell was heard.

There was a pause.

"It would have been a terrible shock to Mrs. Morton if she had been his wife," observed Mr. Blackwell.  "But I suppose persons of that kind have very little feeling.  I must say that it was fortunate for the family that the event happened before Mr. Beaufort was wheedled into so improper a marriage."

"It was fortunate, Blackwell. Have you ordered the post-horses? I shall start immediately after the funeral."

"What is to be done with the cottage, sir?"

"You may advertise it for sale."

"And Mrs. Morton and the boys?" "Hum! we will consider. She was a tradesman's daughter. I think I ought to provide for her suitably, eh?"

"It is more than the world could expect from you, sir; it is very different from a wife."

"Oh, very!--very much so, indeed! Just ring for a lighted candle, we will seal up these boxes. And--I think I could take a sandwich. Poor Philip!"

The funeral was over; the dead shovelled away. What a strange thing it does seem, that that very form which we prized so charily, for which we prayed the winds to be gentle, which we lapped from the cold in our arms, from whose footstep we would have removed a stone, should be suddenly thrust out of sight--an abomination that the earth must not look upon--a despicable loathsomeness, to be concealed and to be forgotten! And this same composition of bone and muscle that was yesterday so strong--which men respected, and women loved, and children clung to--to-day so lamentably powerless, unable to defend or protect those who lay nearest to its heart; its riches wrested from it, its wishes spat upon, its influence expiring with its last sigh! A breath from its lips making all that mighty difference between what it was and what it is!

The post-horses were at the door as the funeral procession returned to the house.

Mr. Robert Beaufort bowed slightly to Mrs. Morton, and said, with his pocket-handkerchief still before his eyes:

"I will write to you in a few days, ma'am; you will find that I shall not forget you. The cottage will be sold; but we sha'n't hurry you. Good-bye, ma'am; good-bye, my boys;" and he patted his nephews on the head.

Philip winced aside, and scowled haughtily at his uncle, who muttered to himself, "That boy will come to no good!" Little Sidney put his hand into the rich man's, and looked up, pleadingly, into his face. "Can't you say something pleasant to poor mamma, Uncle Robert?"

Mr. Beaufort hemmed huskily, and entered the britska--it had been his brother's: the lawyer followed, and they drove away.

A week after the funeral, Philip stole from the house into the conservatory, to gather some fruit for his mother; she had scarcely touched food since Beaufort's death. She was worn to a shadow; her hair had turned grey. Now she had at last found tears, and she wept noiselessly but unceasingly.

The boy had plucked some grapes, and placed them carefully in his basket: he was about to select a nectarine that seemed riper than the rest, when his hand was roughly seized; and the gruff voice of John Green, the gardener, exclaimed:

"What are you about, Master Philip? you must not touch them 'ere fruit!"

"How dare you, fellow!" cried the young gentleman, in a tone of equal astonishment and, wrath.

"None of your airs, Master Philip! What I means is, that some great folks are coming too look at the place tomorrow; and I won't have my show of fruit spoiled by being pawed about by the like of you; so, that's plain, Master Philip!"

The boy grew very pale, but remained silent. The gardener, delighted to retaliate the insolence he had received, continued:

"You need not go for to look so spiteful, master; you are not the great man you thought you were; you are nobody now, and so you will find ere long. So, march out, if you please: I wants to lock up the glass."

As he spoke, he took the lad roughly by the arm; but Philip, the most irascible of mortals, was strong for his years, and fearless as a young lion. He caught up a watering-pot, which the gardener had deposited while he expostulated with his late tyrant and struck the man across the face with it so violently and so suddenly, that he fell back over the beds, and the glass crackled and shivered under him. Philip did not wait for the foe to recover his equilibrium; but, taking up his grapes, and possessing himself quietly of the disputed nectarine, quitted the spot; and the gardener did not think it prudent to pursue him. To boys, under ordinary circumstances--boys who have buffeted their way through a scolding nursery, a wrangling family, or a public school--there would have been nothing in this squabble to dwell on the memory or vibrate on the nerves, after the first burst of passion: but to Philip Beaufort it was an era in life; it was the first insult he had ever received; it was his initiation into that changed, rough, and terrible career, to which the spoiled darling of vanity and love was henceforth condemned. His pride and his self-esteem had incurred a fearful shock. He entered the house, and a sickness came over him; his limbs trembled; he sat down in the hall, and, placing the fruit beside him, covered his face with his hands and wept. Those were not the tears of a boy, drawn from a shallow source; they were the burning, agonising, reluctant tears, that men shed, wrung from the heart as if it were its blood. He had never been sent to school, lest he should meet with mortification. He had had various tutors, trained to show, rather than to exact, respect; one succeeding another, at his own whim and caprice. His natural quickness, and a very strong, hard, inquisitive turn of mind, had enabled him, however, to pick up more knowledge, though of a desultory and miscellaneous nature, than boys of his age generally possess; and his roving, independent, out-of-door existence had served to ripen his understanding. He had certainly, in spite of every precaution, arrived at some, though not very distinct, notion of his peculiar position; but none of its inconveniences had visited him till that day. He began now to turn his eyes to the future; and vague and dark forebodings--a consciousness of the shelter, the protector, the station, he had lost in his father's death--crept coldly, over him. While thus musing, a ring was heard at the bell; he lifted his head; it was the postman with a letter. Philip hastily rose, and, averting his face, on which the tears were not dried, took the letter; and then, snatching up his little basket of fruit, repaired to his mother's room.

The shutters were half closed on the bright day--oh, what a mockery is there in the smile of the happy sun when it shines on the wretched! Mrs. Morton sat, or rather crouched, in a distant corner; her streaming eyes fixed on vacancy; listless, drooping; a very image of desolate woe; and Sidney was weaving flower-chains at her feet.

"Mamma!--mother!" whispered Philip, as he threw his arms round her neck; "look up! look up!-my heart breaks to see you. Do taste this fruit: you will die too, if you go on thus; and what will become of us--of Sidney?"

Mrs. Morton did look up vaguely into his face, and strove to smile.

"See, too, I have brought you a letter; perhaps good news; shall I break the seal?"

Mrs. Morton shook her head gently, and took the letter--alas! how different from that one which Sidney had placed in her hands not two short weeks since--it was Mr. Robert Beaufort's handwriting. She shuddered, and laid it down. And then there suddenly, and for the first time, flashed across her the sense of her strange position--the dread of the future. What were her sons to be henceforth?

What herself? Whatever the sanctity of her marriage, the law might fail her. At the disposition of Mr. Robert Beaufort the fate of three lives might depend. She gasped for breath; again took up the letter; and hurried over the contents: they ran thus:

"DEAR, MADAM,--Knowing that you must naturally be anxious as to the future prospects of your children and yourself, left by my poor brother destitute of all provision, I take the earliest opportunity which it seems to me that propriety and decorum allow, to apprise you of my intentions. I need not say that, properly speaking, you can have no kind of claim upon the relations of my late brother; nor will I hurt your feelings by those moral reflections which at this season of sorrow cannot, I hope, fail involuntarily to force themselves upon you. Without more than this mere allusion to your peculiar connection with my brother, I may, however, be permitted to add that that connection tended very materially to separate him from the legitimate branches of his family; and in consulting with them as to a provision for you and your children, I find that, besides scruples that are to be respected, some natural degree of soreness exists upon their minds. Out of regard, however, to my poor brother (though I saw very little of him of late years), I am willing to waive those feelings which, as a father and a husband, you may conceive that I share with the rest of my family. You will probably now decide on living with some of your own relations; and that you may not be entirely a burden to them, I beg to say that I shall allow you a hundred a year; paid, if you prefer it, quarterly. You may also select such articles of linen and plate as you require for your own use. With regard to your sons, I have no objection to place them at a grammar-school, and, at a proper age, to apprentice them to any trade suitable to their future station, in the choice of which your own family can give you the best advice. If they conduct themselves properly, they may always depend on my protection. I do not wish to hurry your movements; but it will probably be painful to you to remain longer than you can help in a place crowded with unpleasant recollections; and as the cottage is to be sold-- indeed, my brother-in-law, Lord Lilburne, thinks it would suit him--you will be liable to the interruption of strangers to see it; and your prolonged residence at Fernside, you must be sensible, is rather an obstacle to the sale. I beg to inclose you a draft for L100. to pay any present expenses; and to request, when you are settled, to know where the first quarter shall be paid.

"I shall write to Mr. Jackson (who, I think, is the bailiff) to detail my instructions as to selling the crops, &c., and discharging the servants; so that you may have no further trouble.
    "I am, Madam,
    "Your obedient Servant,
    "ROBERT BEAUFORT.
"Berkeley Square, September 12th, 18--."

The letter fell from Catherine's hands. Her grief was changed to indignation and scorn.

"The insolent!" she exclaimed, with flashing eyes. "This to me!--to me-- the wife, the lawful wife of his brother! the wedded mother of his brother's children!"

"Say that again, mother! again--again!" cried Philip, in a loud voice. "His wife--wedded!"

"I swear it," said Catherine, solemnly. "I kept the secret for your father's sake. Now for yours, the truth must be proclaimed."

"Thank God! thank God!" murmured Philip, in a quivering voice, throwing his arms round his brother, "We have no brand on our names, Sidney."

At those accents, so full of suppressed joy and pride, the mother felt at once all that her son had suspected and concealed. She felt that beneath his haughty and wayward character there had lurked delicate and generous forbearance for her; that from his equivocal position his very faults might have arisen; and a pang of remorse for her long sacrifice of the children to the father shot through her heart. It was followed by a fear, an appalling fear, more painful than the remorse. The proofs that were to clear herself and them! The words of her husband, that last awful morning, rang in her ear. The minister dead; the witness absent; the register lost! But the copy of that register!--the copy! might not that suffice? She groaned, and closed her eyes as if to shut out the future: then starting up, she hurried from the room, and went straight to Beaufort's study. As she laid her hand on the latch of the door, she trembled and drew back. But care for the living was stronger at that moment than even anguish for the dead: she entered the apartment; she passed with a firm step to the bureau. It was locked; Robert Beaufort's seal upon the lock:--on every cupboard, every box, every drawer, the same seal that spoke of rights more valued than her own. But Catherine was not daunted: she turned and saw Philip by her side; she pointed to the bureau in silence; the boy understood the appeal. He left the room, and returned in a few moments with a chisel. The lock was broken: tremblingly and eagerly Catherine ransacked the contents; opened paper after paper, letter after letter, in vain: no certificate, no will, no memorial. Could the brother have abstracted the fatal proof? A word sufficed to explain to Philip what she sought for; and his search was more minute than hers. Every possible receptacle for papers in that room, in the whole house, was explored, and still the search was fruitless.

Three hours afterwards they were in the same room in which Philip had brought Robert Beaufort's letter to his mother. Catherine was seated, tearless, but deadly pale with heart-sickness and dismay.

"Mother," said Philip, "may I now read the letter?" Yes, boy; and decide for us all. She paused, and examined his face as he read. He felt her eye was upon him, and restrained his emotions as he proceeded. When he had done, he lifted his dark gaze upon Catherine's watchful countenance.

"Mother, whether or not we obtain our rights, you will still refuse this man's charity? I am young--a boy; but I am strong and active. I will work for you day and night. I have it in me--I feel it; anything rather than eating his bread."

"Philip! Philip! you are indeed my son; your father's son! And have you no reproach for your mother, who so weakly, so criminally, concealed your birthright, till, alas! discovery may be too late? Oh! reproach me, reproach me! it will be kindness. No! do not kiss me! I cannot bear it. Boy! boy! if as my heart tells me, we fail in proof, do you understand what, in the world's eye, I am; what you are?"

"I do!" said Philip, firmly; and lie fell on his knees at her feet." Whatever others call you, you are a mother, and I your son. You are, in the judgment of Heaven, my father's Wife, and I his Heir."

Catherine bowed her head, and with a gush of tears fell into his arms. Sidney crept up to her, and forced his lips to her cold cheek. "Mamma! what vexes you? Mamma, mamma!"

"Oh, Sidney! Sidney! How like his father! Look at him, Philip! Shall we do right to refuse him even this pittance?  Must he be a beggar too?"

"Never beggar," said Philip, with a pride that showed what hard lessons he had yet to learn.  "The lawful sons of a Beaufort were not born to beg their bread!"

# CHAPTER VI.

"The storm above, and frozen world below.

\*        \*        \*        \*        \*

The olive bough
Faded and cast upon the common wind,
And earth a doveless ark."--LAMAN BLANCHARD.

Mr. Robert Beaufort was generally considered by the world a very worthy man.  He had never committed any excess--never gambled nor incurred debt --nor fallen into the warm errors most common with his sex.  He was a good husband--a careful father--an agreeable neighbour--rather charitable than otherwise, to the poor.  He was honest and methodical in his dealings, and had been known to behave handsomely in different relations of life.  Mr. Robert Beaufort, indeed, always meant to do what was right --in the eyes of the world!  He had no other rule of action but that which the world supplied; his religion was decorum--his sense of honour was regard to opinion.  His heart was a dial to which the world was the sun: when the great eye of the public fell on it, it answered every purpose that a heart could answer; but when that eye was invisible, the dial was mute--a piece of brass and nothing more.

It is just to Robert Beaufort to assure the reader that he wholly disbelieved his brother's story of a private marriage.  He considered that tale, when heard for the first time, as the mere invention (and a shallow one) of a man wishing to make the imprudent step he was about to take as respectable as he could. The careless tone of his brother when speaking upon the subject--his confession that of such a marriage there were no distinct proofs, except a copy of a register (which copy Robert had not found)--made his incredulity natural. He therefore deemed himself under no obligation of delicacy or respect, to a woman through whose means he had very nearly lost a noble succession--a woman who had not even borne his brother's name--a woman whom nobody knew. Had Mrs. Morton been Mrs. Beaufort, and the natural sons legitimate children, Robert Beaufort, supposing their situation of relative power and dependence to have been the same, would have behaved with careful and scrupulous generosity. The world would have said, "Nothing can be handsomer than Mr. Robert Beaufort's conduct!" Nay, if Mrs. Morton had been some divorced wife of birth and connections, he would have made very different dispositions in her favour: he would not have allowed the connections to call him shabby. But here he felt that, all circumstances considered, the world, if it spoke at all (which it would scarce think it worth while to do), would be on his side. An artful woman--low-born, and, of course, low-bred--who wanted to inveigle her rich and careless paramour into marriage; what could be expected from the man she had sought to injure--the rightful heir? Was it not very good in him to do anything for her, and, if he provided for the children suitably to the original station of the mother, did he not go to the very utmost of reasonable expectation? He certainly thought in his conscience, such as it was, that he had acted well--not extravagantly, not foolishly; but well. He was sure the world would say so if it knew all: he was not bound to do anything. He was not, therefore, prepared for Catherine's short, haughty, but temperate reply to his letter: a reply which conveyed a decided refusal of his offers--asserted positively her own marriage, and the claims of her children--intimated legal proceedings--and was signed in the name of Catherine Beaufort. Mr. Beaufort put the letter in his bureau, labelled, "Impertinent answer from Mrs. Morton, Sept. 14," and was quite contented to forget the existence of the writer, until his lawyer, Mr. Blackwell, informed him that a suit had been instituted by Catherine.

Mr. Robert turned pale, but Blackwell composed him.

"Pooh, sir! you have nothing to fear.  It is but an attempt to extort money: the attorney is a low practitioner, accustomed to get up bad cases: they can make nothing of it."

This was true: whatever the rights of the case, poor Catherine had no proofs--no evidence--which could justify a respectable lawyer to advise her proceeding to a suit.  She named two witnesses of her marriage--one dead, the other could not be heard of.  She selected for the alleged place in which the ceremony was performed a very remote village, in which it appeared that the register had been destroyed.  No attested copy thereof was to be found, and Catherine was stunned on hearing that, even if found, it was doubtful whether it could be received as evidence, unless to corroborate actual personal testimony.  It so happened that when Philip, many years ago, had received a copy, he had not shown it to Catherine, nor mentioned Mr. Jones's name as the copyist.  In fact, then only three years married to Catherine, his worldly caution had not yet been conquered by confident experience of her generosity.  As for the mere moral evidence dependent on the publication of her bans in London, that amounted to no proof whatever; nor, on inquiry at A----, did the Welsh villagers remember anything further than that, some fifteen years ago, a handsome gentleman had visited Mr. Price, and one or two rather thought that Mr. Price had married him to a lady from London; evidence quite inadmissible against the deadly, damning fact, that, for fifteen years, Catherine had openly borne another name, and lived with Mr. Beaufort ostensibly as his mistress.  Her generosity in this destroyed her case.  Nevertheless, she found a low practitioner, who took her money and neglected her cause; so her suit was heard and dismissed with contempt.  Henceforth, then, indeed, in the eyes of the law and the public, Catherine was an impudent adventurer, and her sons were nameless outcasts.

And now relieved from all fear, Mr. Robert Beaufort entered upon the full enjoyment of his splendid fortune.

The house in Berkeley Square was furnished anew.  Great dinners and gay routs were given in the ensuing spring.  Mr. and Mrs. Beaufort became persons of considerable importance.  The rich man had, even when poor, been ambitious; his ambition now centred in his only son.  Arthur had always been considered a boy of talents and promise; to what might he not now aspire?  The term of his probation with the tutor was abridged, and Arthur Beaufort was sent at once to Oxford.

Before he went to the university, during a short preparatory visit to his father, Arthur spoke to him of the Mortons. "What has become of them, sir? and what have you done for them?"

"Done for them!" said Mr. Beaufort, opening his eyes. "What should I do for persons who have just been harassing me with the most unprincipled litigation?  My conduct to them has been too generous: that is, all things considered.  But when you are my age you will find there is very little gratitude in the world, Arthur."

"Still, sir," said Arthur, with the good nature that belonged to him: "still, my uncle was greatly attached to them; and the boys, at least, are guiltless."

"Well, well!" replied Mr. Beaufort, a little impatiently; "I believe they want for nothing: I fancy they are with the mother's relations. Whenever they address me in a proper manner they shall not find me revengeful or hardhearted; but, since we are on this topic," continued

the father smoothing his shirt-frill with a care that showed his decorum
even in trifles, "I hope you see the results of that kind of connection,
and that you will take warning by your poor uncle's example. And now let
us change the subject; it is not a very pleasant one, and, at your age,
the less your thoughts turn on such matters the better."

Arthur Beaufort, with the careless generosity of youth, that gauges other
men's conduct by its own sentiments, believed that his father, who had
never been niggardly to himself, had really acted as his words implied;
and, engrossed by the pursuits of the new and brilliant career opened,
whether to his pleasures or his studies, suffered the objects of his
inquiries to pass from his thoughts.

Meanwhile, Mrs. Morton, for by that name we must still call her, and her
children, were settled in a small lodging in a humble suburb; situated on
the high road between Fernside and the metropolis. She saved from her
hopeless law-suit, after the sale of her jewels and ornaments, a
sufficient sum to enable her, with economy, to live respectably for a
year or two at least, during which time she might arrange her plans for
the future. She reckoned, as a sure resource, upon the assistance of her
relations; but it was one to which she applied with natural shame and
reluctance. She had kept up a correspondence with her father during his
life. To him, she never revealed the secret of her marriage, though she
did not write like a person conscious of error. Perhaps, as she always
said to her son, she had made to her husband a solemn promise never to
divulge or even hint that secret until he himself should authorise its
disclosure. For neither he nor Catherine ever contemplated separation or
death. Alas! how all of us, when happy, sleep secure in the dark
shadows, which ought to warn us of the sorrows that are to come! Still
Catherine's father, a man of coarse mind and not rigid principles, did
not take much to heart that connection which he assumed to be illicit.
She was provided for, that was some comfort: doubtless Mr. Beaufort would
act like a gentleman, perhaps at last make her an honest woman and a

lady. Meanwhile, she had a fine house, and a fine carriage, and fine servants; and so far from applying to him for money, was constantly sending him little presents. But Catherine only saw, in his permission of her correspondence, kind, forgiving, and trustful affection, and she loved him tenderly: when he died, the link that bound her to her family was broken. Her brother succeeded to the trade; a man of probity and honour, but somewhat hard and unamiable. In the only letter she had received from him--the one announcing her father's death--he told her plainly, and very properly, that he could not countenance the life she led; that he had children growing up--that all intercourse between them was at an end, unless she left Mr. Beaufort; when, if she sincerely repented, he would still prove her affectionate brother.

Though Catherine had at the time resented this letter as unfeeling--now, humbled and sorrow-stricken, she recognised the propriety of principle from which it emanated. Her brother was well off for his station--she would explain to him her real situation--he would believe her story. She would write to him, and beg him at least to give aid to her poor children.

But this step she did not take till a considerable portion of her pittance was consumed--till nearly three parts of a year since Beaufort's death had expired--and till sundry warnings, not to be lightly heeded, had made her forebode the probability of an early death for herself. From the age of sixteen, when she had been placed by Mr. Beaufort at the head of his household, she had been cradled, not in extravagance, but in an easy luxury, which had not brought with it habits of economy and thrift. She could grudge anything to herself, but to her children--his children, whose every whim had been anticipated, she had not the heart to be saving. She could have starved in a garret had she been alone; but she could not see them wanting a comfort while she possessed a guinea. Philip, to do him justice, evinced a consideration not to have been expected from his early and arrogant recklessness. But Sidney, who could expect consideration from such a child?  What could he know of the change of circumstances--of the value of money?  Did he seem dejected, Catherine would steal out and spend a week's income on the lapful of toys which she brought home.  Did he seem a shade more pale--did he complain of the slightest ailment, a doctor must be sent for.  Alas! her own ailments, neglected and unheeded, were growing beyond the reach of medicine.  Anxious fearful--gnawed by regret for the past--the thought of famine in the future--she daily fretted and wore herself away.  She had cultivated her mind during her secluded residence with Mr. Beaufort, but she had learned none of the arts by which decayed gentlewomen keep the wolf from the door; no little holiday accomplishments, which, in the day of need turn to useful trade; no water-colour drawings, no paintings on velvet, no fabrications of pretty gewgaws, no embroidery and fine needlework. She was helpless--utterly helpless; if she had resigned herself to the thought of service, she would not have had the physical strength for a place of drudgery, and where could she have found the testimonials necessary for a place of trust?  A great change, at this time, was apparent in Philip.  Had he fallen, then, into kind hands, and under guiding eyes, his passions and energies might have ripened into rare qualities and great virtues.  But perhaps as Goethe has somewhere said, "Experience, after all, is the best teacher."  He kept a constant guard on his vehement temper--his wayward will; he would not have vexed his mother for the world.  But, strange to say (it was a great mystery in the woman's heart), in proportion as he became more amiable, it seemed that his mother loved him less.  Perhaps she did not, in that change, recognise so closely the darling of the old time; perhaps the very weaknesses and importunities of Sidney, the hourly sacrifices the child entailed upon her, endeared the younger son more to her from that natural sense of dependence and protection which forms the great bond between mother and child; perhaps too, as Philip had been one to inspire as much pride as affection, so the pride faded away with the expectations that had fed it, and carried off in its decay some of the affection that was intertwined with it.  However this be, Philip had formerly appeared the more spoiled and favoured of the two: and now Sidney seemed all in all. Thus, beneath the younger son's caressing gentleness, there grew up a certain regard for self; it was latent, it took amiable colours; it had even a certain charm and grace in so sweet a child, but selfishness it was not the less. In this he differed from his brother. Philip was self-willed: Sidney self-loving. A certain timidity of character, endearing perhaps to the anxious heart of a mother, made this fault in the younger boy more likely to take root. For, in bold natures, there is a lavish and uncalculating recklessness which scorns self unconsciously and though there is a fear which arises from a loving heart, and is but sympathy for others--the fear which belongs to a timid character is but egotism--but, when physical, the regard for one's own person: when moral, the anxiety for one's own interests.

It was in a small room in a lodging-house in the suburb of H---- that Mrs. Morton was seated by the window, nervously awaiting the knock of the postman, who was expected to bring her brother's reply to her letter. It was therefore between ten and eleven o'clock--a morning in the merry month of June. It was hot and sultry, which is rare in an English June. A flytrap, red, white, and yellow, suspended from the ceiling, swarmed with flies; flies were on the ceiling, flies buzzed at the windows; the sofa and chairs of horsehair seemed stuffed with flies. There was an air of heated discomfort in the thick, solid moreen curtains, in the gaudy paper, in the bright-staring carpet, in the very looking-glass over the chimney-piece, where a strip of mirror lay imprisoned in an embrace of frame covered with yellow muslin. We may talk of the dreariness of winter; and winter, no doubt, is desolate: but what in the world is more dreary to eyes inured to the verdure and bloom of Nature--,

"The pomp of groves and garniture of fields,"

--than a close room in a suburban lodging-house; the sun piercing every corner; nothing fresh, nothing cool, nothing fragrant to be seen, felt, or inhaled; all dust, glare, noise, with a chandler's shop, perhaps, next door?  Sidney armed with a pair of scissors, was cutting the pictures out of a story-book, which his mother had bought him the day before.  Philip, who, of late, had taken much to rambling about the streets--it may be, in hopes of meeting one of those benevolent, eccentric, elderly gentlemen, he had read of in old novels, who suddenly come to the relief of distressed virtue; or, more probably, from the restlessness that belonged to his adventurous temperament;--Philip had left the house since breakfast.

"Oh! how hot this nasty room is!" exclaimed Sidney, abruptly, looking up from his employment.  "Sha'n't we ever go into the country, again, mamma?"

"Not at present, my love."

"I wish I could have my pony; why can't I have my pony, mamma?"

"Because,--because--the pony is sold, Sidney."

"Who sold it?"

"Your uncle."

"He is a very naughty man, my uncle: is he not?  But can't I have another pony?  It would be so nice, this fine weather!"

"Ah! my dear, I wish I could afford it: but you shall have a ride this week!  Yes," continued the mother, as if reasoning with herself, in excuse of the extravagance, "he does not look well: poor child! he must have exercise."

"A ride!--oh! that is my own kind mamma!" exclaimed Sidney, clapping his hands. "Not on a donkey, you know!--a pony. The man down the street, there, lets ponies. I must have the white pony with the long tail. But, I say, mamma, don't tell Philip, pray don't; he would be jealous."

"No, not jealous, my dear; why do you think so?"

"Because he is always angry when I ask you for anything. It is very unkind in him, for I don't care if he has a pony, too,--only not the white one."

Here the postman's knock, loud and sudden, started Mrs. Morton from her seat.

She pressed her hands tightly to her heart, as if to still its beating, and went tremulously to the door; thence to the stairs, to anticipate the lumbering step of the slipshod maidservent.

"Give it me, Jane; give it me!"

"One shilling and eightpence--double charged--if you please, ma'am! Thank you."

"Mamma, may I tell Jane to engage the pony?"

"Not now, my love; sit down; be quiet: I--I am not well."

Sidney, who was affectionate and obedient, crept back peaceably to the window, and, after a short, impatient sigh, resumed the scissors and the story-book. I do not apologise to the reader for the various letters I am obliged to lay before him; for character often betrays itself more in letters than in speech. Mr. Roger Morton's reply was couched in these terms,--

"DEAR CATHERINE, I have received your letter of the 14th inst., and write per return.  I am very much grieved to hear of your afflictions; but, whatever you say, I cannot think the late Mr. Beaufort acted like a conscientious man, in forgetting to make his will, and leaving his little ones destitute.  It is all very well to talk of his intentions; but the proof of the pudding is in the eating.  And it is hard upon me, who have a large family of my own, and get my livelihood by honest industry, to have a rich gentleman's children to maintain.  As for your story about the private marriage, it may or not be.  Perhaps you were taken in by that worthless man, for a real marriage it could not be.  And, as you say, the law has decided that point; therefore, the less you say on the matter the better.  It all comes to the same thing.  People are not bound to believe what can't be proved.  And even if what you say is true, you are more to be blamed than pitied for holding your tongue so many years, and discrediting an honest family, as ours has always been considered.  I am sure my wife would not have thought of such a thing for the finest gentleman that ever wore shoe-leather.  However, I don't want to hurt your feelings; and I am sure I am ready to do whatever is right and proper.  You cannot expect that I should ask you to my house.  My wife, you know, is a very religious woman--what is called evangelical; but that's neither here nor there: I deal with all people, churchmen and dissenters--even Jews,--and don't trouble my head much about differences in opinion.  I dare say there are many ways to heaven; as I said, the other day, to Mr. Thwaites, our member.  But it is right to say my wife will not hear of your coming here; and, indeed, it might do harm to my business, for there are several elderly single gentlewomen, who buy flannel for the poor at my shop, and they are very particular; as they ought to be, indeed: for morals are very strict in this county, and particularly in this town, where we certainly do pay very high church-rates.  Not that I grumble; for, though I am as liberal as any man, I am for an established church; as I ought to be, since the dean is my best customer.  With regard to yourself I inclose you L10., and you will let me know when it is gone, and I will see what more I can do.  You say you are very poorly, which I am sorry to hear; but you must pluck up your spirits, and take in plain work; and I really think you ought to apply to Mr. Robert Beaufort. He bears a high character; and notwithstanding your lawsuit, which I cannot approve of, I dare say he might allow you L40. or L50. a-year, if you apply properly, which would be the right thing in him. So much for you. As for the boys--poor, fatherless creatures!--it is very hard that they should be so punished for no fault of their own; and my wife, who, though strict, is a good-hearted woman, is ready and willing to do what I wish about them. You say the eldest is near sixteen and well come on in his studies. I can get him a very good thing in a light genteel way. My wife's brother, Mr. Christopher Plaskwith, is a bookseller and stationer with pretty practice, in R----. He is a clever man, and has a newspaper, which he kindly sends me every week; and, though it is not my county, it has some very sensible views and is often noticed in the London papers, as 'our provincial contemporary.'--Mr. Plaskwith owes me some money, which I advanced him when he set up the paper; and he has several times most honestly offered to pay me, in shares in the said paper. But, as the thing might break, and I don't like concerns I don't understand, I have not taken advantage of his very handsome proposals. Now, Plaskwith wrote me word, two days ago, that he wanted a genteel, smart lad, as assistant and 'prentice, and offered to take my eldest boy; but we can't spare him. I write to Christopher by this post; and if your youth will run down on the top of the coach, and inquire for Mr. Plaskwith--the fare is trifling--I have no doubt he will be engaged at once. But you will say, 'There's the premium to consider!' No such thing; Kit will set off the premium against his debt to me; so you will have nothing to pay. 'Tis a very pretty business; and the lad's education will get him on; so that's off your mind. As to the little chap, I'll take him at once. You say he is a pretty boy; and a pretty boy is always a help in a linendraper's shop. He shall share and share with my own young folks; and Mrs. Morton will take care of his washing and morals. I conclude--(this is Mrs. M's. suggestion)--that he has had the measles, cowpock, and whooping-cough, which please let me know. If

he behave well, which, at his age, we can easily break him into, he is
settled for life.  So now you have got rid of two mouths to feed, and
have nobody to think of but yourself, which must be a great comfort.
Don't forget to write to Mr. Beaufort; and if he don't do something for
you he's not the gentleman I take him for; but you are my own flesh and
blood, and sha'n't starve; for, though I don't think it right in a man in
business to encourage what's wrong, yet, when a person's down in the
world, I think an ounce of hell is better than a pound of preaching.  My
wife thinks otherwise, and wants to send you some tracts; but every
body can't be as correct as some folks.  However, as I said before,
that's neither here nor there.  Let me know when your boy comes down, and
also about the measles, cowpock, and whooping-cough; also if all's right
with Mr. Plaskwith.  So now I hope you will feel more comfortable; and
remain,

> "Dear Catherine,
> "Your forgiving and affectionate brother,
> "ROGER MORTON.

"High Street, N----, June 13."


"P.S.--Mrs. M. says that she will be a mother to your little boy, and
that you had better mend up all his linen before you send him."


As Catherine finished this epistle, she lifted her eyes and beheld
Philip.  He had entered noiselessly, and he remained silent, leaning
against the wall, and watching the face of his mother, which crimsoned
with painful humiliation while she read.  Philip was not now the trim and
dainty stripling first introduced to the reader.  He had outgrown his
faded suit of funereal mourning; his long-neglected hair hung elf-like
and matted down his cheeks; there was a gloomy look in his bright dark
eyes.  Poverty never betrays itself more than in the features and form of
Pride.  It was evident that his spirit endured, rather than accommodated
itself to, his fallen state; and, notwithstanding his soiled and

threadbare garments, and a haggardness that ill becomes the years of palmy youth, there was about his whole mien and person a wild and savage grandeur more impressive than his former ruffling arrogance of manner.

"Well, mother," said he, with a strange mixture of sternness in his countenance and pity in his voice; "well, mother, and what says your brother?"

"You decided for us once before, decide again. But I need not ask you; you would never--"

"I don't know," interrupted Philip, vaguely; "let me see what we are to decide on."

Mrs. Morton was naturally a woman of high courage and spirit, but sickness and grief had worn down both; and though Philip was but sixteen, there is something in the very nature of woman--especially in trouble-- which makes her seek to lean on some other will than her own. She gave Philip the letter, and went quietly to sit down by Sidney.

"Your brother means well," said Philip, when he had concluded the epistle.

"Yes, but nothing is to be done; I cannot, cannot send poor Sidney to-- to--" and Mrs. Morton sobbed.

"No, my dear, dear mother, no; it would be terrible, indeed, to part you and him. But this bookseller--Plaskwith--perhaps I shall be able to support you both."

"Why, you do not think, Philip, of being an apprentice!--you, who have been so brought up--you, who are so proud!"

"Mother, I would sweep the crossings for your sake I Mother, for your sake I would go to my uncle Beaufort with my hat in my hand, for halfpence. Mother, I am not proud--I would be honest, if I can--but when I see you pining away, and so changed, the devil comes into me, and I often shudder lest I should commit some crime--what, I don't know!"

"Come here, Philip--my own Philip--my son, my hope, my firstborn!"--and the mother's heart gushed forth in all the fondness of early days. "Don't speak so terribly, you frighten me!"

She threw her arms round his neck, and kissed him soothingly. He laid his burning temples on her bosom, and nestled himself to her, as he had been wont to do, after some stormy paroxysm of his passionate and wayward infancy. So there they remained--their lips silent, their hearts speaking to each other--each from each taking strange succour and holy strength--till Philip rose, calm, and with a quiet smile, "Good-bye, mother; I will go at once to Mr. Plaskwith."

"But you have no money for the coach-fare; here, Philip," and she placed her purse in his hand, from which he reluctantly selected a few shillings. "And mind, if the man is rude and you dislike him--mind, you must not subject yourself to insolence and mortification."

"Oh, all will go well, don't fear," said Philip, cheerfully, and he left the house.

Towards evening he had reached his destination. The shop was of goodly exterior, with a private entrance; over the shop was written, "Christopher Plaskwith, Bookseller and Stationer:" on the private door a brass plate, inscribed with "R---- and ---- Mercury Office, Mr. Plaskwith." Philip applied at the private entrance, and was shown by a "neat-handed Phillis" into a small office-room. In a few minutes the door opened, and the bookseller entered.

Mr. Christopher Plaskwith was a short, stout man, in drab-coloured breeches, and gaiters to match; a black coat and waistcoat; he wore a large watch-chain, with a prodigious bunch of seals, alternated by small keys and old-fashioned mourning-rings.  His complexion was pale and sodden, and his hair short, dark, and sleek.  The bookseller valued himself on a likeness to Buonaparte; and affected a short, brusque, peremptory manner, which he meant to be the indication of the vigorous and decisive character of his prototype.

"So you are the young gentleman Mr. Roger Morton recommends?"  Here Mr. Plaskwith took out a huge pocketbook, slowly unclasped it, staring hard at Philip, with what he designed for a piercing and penetrative survey.

"This is the letter--no! this is Sir Thomas Champerdown's order for fifty copies of the last Mercury, containing his speech at the county meeting. Your age, young man?--only sixteen?--look older;--that's not it--that's not it--and this is it!--sit down.  Yes, Mr. Roger Morton recommends you --a relation--unfortunate circumstances--well educated--hum!  Well, young man, what have you to say for yourself?"

"Sir?"

"Can you cast accounts?--know bookkeeping?"

"I know something of algebra, sir."

"Algebra!--oh, what else?"

"French and Latin."

"Hum!--may be useful.  Why do you wear your hair so long?--look at mine. What's your name?"

"Philip Morton."

"Mr. Philip Morton, you have an intelligent countenance--I go a great deal by countenances. You know the terms?--most favourable to you. No premium--I settle that with Roger. I give board and bed--find your own washing. Habits regular--'prenticeship only five years; when over, must not set up in the same town. I will see to the indentures. When can you come?"

"When you please, sir."

"Day after to-morrow, by six o'clock coach."

"But, sir," said Philip, "will there be no salary? something, ever so small, that I could send to my another?"

"Salary, at sixteen?--board and bed-no premium! Salary, what for? 'Prentices have no salary!--you will have every comfort."

"Give me less comfort, that I may give my mother more;--a little money, ever so little, and take it out of my board: I can do with one meal a day, sir."

The bookseller was moved: he took a huge pinch of snuff out of his waistcoat pocket, and mused a moment. He then said, as he re-examined Philip:

"Well, young man, I'll tell you what we will do. You shall come here first upon trial;--see if we like each other before we sign the indentures; allow you, meanwhile, five shillings a week. If you show talent, will see if I and Roger can settle about some little allowance. That do, eh?"

"I thank you, sir, yes," said Philip, gratefully. "Agreed, then. Follow me--present you to Mrs. P." Thus saying, Mr. Plaskwith returned the letter to the pocket-book, and the pocket-book to the pocket; and, putting his arms behind his coat tails, threw up his chin, and strode through the passage into a small parlour, that locked upon a small garden. Here, seated round the table, were a thin lady, with a squint (Mrs. Plaskwith), two little girls, the Misses Plaskwith, also with squints, and pinafores; a young man of three or four-and-twenty, in nankeen trousers, a little the worse for washing, and a black velveteen jacket and waistcoat. This young gentleman was very much freckled; wore his hair, which was dark and wiry, up at one side, down at the other; had a short thick nose; full lips; and, when close to him, smelt of cigars. Such was Mr. Plimmins, Mr. Plaskwith's factotum, foreman in the shop, assistant editor to the Mercury. Mr. Plaskwith formally went the round of the introduction; Mrs. P. nodded her head; the Misses P. nudged each other, and grinned; Mr. Plimmins passed his hand through his hair, glanced at the glass, and bowed very politely.

"Now, Mrs. P., my second cup, and give Mr. Morton his dish of tea. Must be tired, sir--hot day. Jemima, ring--no, go to the stairs and call out 'more buttered toast.' That's the shorter way--promptitude is my rule in life, Mr. Morton. Pray-hum, hum--have you ever, by chance, studied the biography of the great Napoleon Buonaparte?"

Mr. Plimmins gulped down his tea, and kicked Philip under the table. Philip looked fiercely at the foreman, and replied, sullenly, "No, sir."

"That's a pity. Napoleon Buonaparte was a very great man,--very! You have seen his cast?--there it is, on the dumb waiter! Look at it! see a likeness, eh?"

"Likeness, sir? I never saw Napoleon Buonaparte."

"Never saw him! No, just look round the room. Who does that bust put you in mind of? who does it resemble?"

Here Mr. Plaskwith rose, and placed himself in an attitude; his hand in his waistcoat, and his face pensively inclined towards the tea-table. "Now fancy me at St. Helena; this table is the ocean. Now, then, who is that cast like, Mr. Philip Morton?"

"I suppose, sir, it is like you!"

"Ah, that it is! strikes every one! Does it not, Mrs. P., does it not? And when you have known me longer, you will find a moral similitude--a moral, sir! Straightforward--short--to the point--bold--determined!"

"Bless me, Mr. P.!" said Mrs. Plaskwith, very querulously, "do make haste with your tea; the young gentleman, I suppose, wants to go home, and the coach passes in a quarter of an hour."

"Have you seen Kean in Richard the Third, Mr. Morton?" asked Mr. Plimmins.

"I have never seen a play."

"Never seen a play! How very odd!"

"Not at all odd, Mr. Plimmins," said the stationer. "Mr. Morton has known troubles--so hand him the hot toast."

Silent and morose, but rather disdainful than sad, Philip listened to the babble round him, and observed the ungenial characters with which he was to associate. He cared not to please (that, alas! had never been especially his study); it was enough for him if he could see, stretching to his mind's eye beyond the walls of that dull room, the long vistas into fairer fortune. At sixteen, what sorrow can freeze the Hope, or what prophetic fear whisper, "Fool!" to the Ambition? He would bear back into ease and prosperity, if not into affluence and station, the dear ones left at home. From the eminence of five shillings a week, he looked over the Promised Land.

At length, Mr. Plaskwith, pulling out his watch, said, "Just in time to catch the coach; make your bow and be off-smart's the word!" Philip rose, took up his hat, made a stiff bow that included the whole group, and vanished with his host.

Mrs. Plaskwith breathed more easily when he was gone. "I never seed a more odd, fierce, ill-bred-looking young man! I declare I am quite afraid of him. What an eye he has!"

"Uncommonly dark; what I may say gipsy-like," said Mr. Plimmins.

"He! he! You always do say such good things, Plimmins. Gipsy-like, he! he! So he is! I wonder if be can tell fortunes?"

"He'll be long before he has a fortune of his own to tell. Ha! ha!" said Plimmins.

"He! he! how very good! you are so pleasant, Plimmins."

While these strictures on his appearance were still going on, Philip had already ascended the roof of the coach; and, waving his hand, with the condescension of old times, to his future master, was carried away by the "Express" in a whirlwind of dust.

"A very warm evening, sir," said a passenger seated at his right; puffing, while he spoke, from a short German pipe, a volume of smoke in

Philip's face.

"Very warm.  Be so good as to smoke into the face of the gentleman on the other side of you," returned Philip, petulantly.

"Ho, ho!" replied the passenger, with a loud, powerful laugh-the laugh of a strong man.  "You don't take to the pipe yet; you will by and by, when you have known the cares and anxieties that I have gone through.  A pipe! --it is a great soother!--a pleasant comforter!  Blue devils fly before its honest breath!  It ripens the brain--it opens the heart; and the man who smokes thinks like a sage and acts like a Samaritan!"

Roused from his reverie by this quaint and unexpected declamation, Philip turned his quick glance at his neighbour.  He saw a man of great bulk and immense physical power--broad-shouldered--deep-chested--not corpulent, but taking the same girth from bone and muscle that a corpulent man does from flesh.  He wore a blue coat--frogged, braided, and buttoned to the throat.  A broad-brimmed straw hat, set on one side, gave a jaunty appearance to a countenance which, notwithstanding its jovial complexion and smiling mouth, had, in repose, a bold and decided character.  It was a face well suited to the frame, inasmuch as it betokened a mind capable of wielding and mastering the brute physical force of body;--light eyes of piercing intelligence; rough, but resolute and striking features, and a jaw of iron.  There was thought, there was power, there was passion in the shaggy brow, the deep-ploughed lines, the dilated, nostril and the restless play of the lips.  Philip looked hard and grave, and the man returned his look.

"What do you think of me, young gentleman?" asked the passenger, as he replaced the pipe in his mouth.  "I am a fine-looking man, am I not?"

"You seem a strange one."

"Strange!--Ay, I puzzle you, as I have done, and shall do, many. You cannot read me as easily as I can read you. Come, shall I guess at your character and circumstances? You are a gentleman, or something like it, by birth;--that the tone of your voice tells me. You are poor, devilish poor;--that the hole in your coat assures me. You are proud, fiery, discontented, and unhappy;--all that I see in your face. It was because I saw those signs that I spoke to you. I volunteer no acquaintance with the happy."

"I dare say not; for if you know all the unhappy you must have a sufficiently large acquaintance," returned Philip.

"Your wit is beyond your years! What is your calling, if the question does not offend you?"

"I have none as yet," said Philip, with a slight sigh, and a deep blush.

"More's the pity!" grunted the smoker, with a long emphatic nasal intonation. "I should have judged that you were a raw recruit in the camp of the enemy."

"Enemy! I don't understand you."

"In other words, a plant growing out of a lawyer's desk. I will explain. There is one class of spiders, industrious, hard-working octopedes, who, out of the sweat of their brains (I take it, by the by, that a spider must have a fine craniological development), make their own webs and catch their flies. There is another class of spiders who have no stuff in them wherewith to make webs; they, therefore, wander about, looking out for food provided by the toil of their neighbours. Whenever they come to the web of a smaller spider, whose larder seems well supplied, they rush upon his domain--pursue him to his hole--eat him up if they can--reject him if he is too tough for their maws, and quietly possess themselves of all the legs and wings they find dangling in his meshes: these spiders I call enemies--the world calls them lawyers!"

Philip laughed: "And who are the first class of spiders?"

"Honest creatures who openly confess that they live upon flies. Lawyers fall foul upon them, under pretence of delivering flies from their clutches. They are wonderful blood-suckers, these lawyers, in spite of all their hypocrisy. Ha! ha! ho! ho!"

And with a loud, rough chuckle, more expressive of malignity than mirth, the man turned himself round, applied vigorously to his pipe, and sank into a silence which, as mile after mile glided past the wheels, he did not seem disposed to break. Neither was Philip inclined to be communicative. Considerations for his own state and prospects swallowed up the curiosity he might otherwise have felt as to his singular neighbour. He had not touched food since the early morning. Anxiety had made him insensible to hunger, till he arrived at Mr. Plaskwith's; and then, feverish, sore, and sick at heart, the sight of the luxuries gracing the tea-table only revolted him. He did not now feel hunger, but he was fatigued and faint. For several nights the sleep which youth can so ill dispense with had been broken and disturbed; and now, the rapid motion of the coach, and the free current of a fresher and more exhausting air than he had been accustomed to for many months, began to operate on his nerves like the intoxication of a narcotic. His eyes grew heavy; indistinct mists, through which there seemed to glare the various squints of the female Plaskwiths, succeeded the gliding road and the dancing trees. His head fell on his bosom; and thence, instinctively seeking the strongest support at hand, inclined towards the stout smoker, and finally nestled itself composedly on that gentleman's shoulder. The passenger, feeling this unwelcome and unsolicited weight, took the pipe, which he had already thrice refilled, from his lips, and emitted an angry and impatient snort; finding that this produced no effect, and that the

load grew heavier as the boy's sleep grew deeper, he cried, in a loud
voice, "Holla! I did not pay my fare to be your bolster, young man!" and
shook himself lustily. Philip started, and would have fallen sidelong
from the coach, if his neighbour had not griped him hard with a hand that
could have kept a young oak from falling.

"Rouse yourself!--you might have had an ugly tumble." Philip muttered
something inaudible, between sleeping and waking, and turned his dark
eyes towards the man; in that glance there was so much unconscious, but
sad and deep reproach, that the passenger felt touched and ashamed.
Before however, he could say anything in apology or conciliation, Philip
had again fallen asleep. But this time, as if he had felt and resented
the rebuff he had received, he inclined his head away from his neighbour,
against the edge of a box on the roof--a dangerous pillow, from which any
sudden jolt might transfer him to the road below.

"Poor lad!--he looks pale!" muttered the man, and he knocked the weed
from his pipe, which he placed gently in his pocket. "Perhaps the smoke
was too much for him--he seems ill and thin," and he took the boy's long
lean fingers in his own. "His cheek is hollow!--what do I know but it
may be with fasting? Pooh! I was a brute. Hush, coachee, hush! don't
talk so loud, and be d---d to you--he will certainly be off!" and the
man softly and creepingly encircled the boy's waist with his huge arm.

"Now, then, to shift his head; so-so,--that's right." Philip's sallow
cheek and long hair were now tenderly lapped on the soliloquist's bosom.
"Poor wretch! he smiles; perhaps he is thinking of home, and the
butterflies he ran after when he was an urchin--they never come back,
those days;--never--never--never! I think the wind veers to the east; he
may catch cold;"--and with that, the man, sliding the head for a moment,
and with the tenderness of a woman, from his breast to his shoulder,
unbuttoned his coat (as he replaced the weight, no longer unwelcomed, in
its former part), and drew the lappets closely round the slender frame of

the sleeper, exposing his own sturdy breast--for he wore no waistcoat--to the sharpening air.  Thus cradled on that stranger's bosom, wrapped from the present and dreaming perhaps--while a heart scorched by fierce and terrible struggles with life and sin made his pillow--of a fair and unsullied future, slept the fatherless and friendless boy.

# CHAPTER VII.

"*Constance*.  My life, my joy, my food, my all the world,
My widow-comfort."--King John.

Amidst the glare of lamps--the rattle of carriages--the lumbering of carts and waggons--the throng, the clamour, the reeking life and dissonant roar of London, Philip woke from his happy sleep.  He woke uncertain and confused, and saw strange eyes bent on him kindly and watchfully.

"You have slept well, my lad!" said the passenger, in the deep ringing voice which made itself heard above all the noises around.

"And you have suffered me to incommode you thus!" said Philip, with more gratitude in his voice and look than, perhaps, he had shown to any one out of his own family since his birth.

"You have had but little kindness shown you, my poor boy, if you think so much of this."

"No--all people were very kind to me once.  I did not value it then."
Here the coach rolled heavily down the dark arch of the inn-yard.

"Take care of yourself, my boy! You look ill;" and in the dark the man slipped a sovereign into Philip's hand.

"I don't want money. Though I thank you heartily all the same; it would be a shame at my age to be a beggar. But can you think of an employment where I can make something?--what they offer me is so trifling. I have a mother and a brother--a mere child, sir--at home."

"Employment!" repeated the man; and as the coach now stopped at the tavern door, the light of the lamp fell full on his marked face. "Ay, I know of employment; but you should apply to some one else to obtain it for you! As for me, it is not likely that we shall meet again!"

"I am sorry for that!--What and who are you?" asked Philip, with a rude and blunt curiosity.

"Me!" returned the passenger, with his deep laugh. "Oh! I know some people who call me an honest fellow. Take the employment offered you, no matter how trifling the wages--keep out of harm's way. Good night to you!"

So saying, he quickly descended from the roof, and, as he was directing the coachman where to look for his carpetbag, Philip saw three or four well-dressed men make up to him, shake him heartily by the hand, and welcome him with great seeming cordiality.

Philip sighed. "He has friends," he muttered to himself; and, paying his fare, he turned from the bustling yard, and took his solitary way home.

A week after his visit to R----, Philip was settled on his probation at Mr. Plaskwith's, and Mrs. Morton's health was so decidedly worse, that she resolved to know her fate, and consult a physician. The oracle was at first ambiguous in its response. But when Mrs. Morton said firmly,

"I have duties to perform; upon your candid answer rest my Plans with respect to my children--left, if I die suddenly, destitute in the world,"--the doctor looked hard in her face, saw its calm resolution, and replied frankly:

"Lose no time, then, in arranging your plans; life is uncertain with all --with you, especially; you may live some time yet, but your constitution is much shaken--I fear there is water on the chest. No, ma'am-no fee. I will see you again."

The physician turned to Sidney, who played with his watch-chain, and smiled up in his face.

"And that child, sir?" said the mother, wistfully, forgetting the dread fiat pronounced against herself,--"he is so delicate!"

"Not at all, ma'am,--a very fine little fellow;" and the doctor patted the boy's head, and abruptly vanished.

"Ah! mamma, I wish you would ride--I wish you would take the white pony!"

"Poor boy! poor boy!" muttered the mother; "I must not be selfish." She covered her face with her hands, and began to think!

Could she, thus doomed, resolve on declining her brother's offer? Did it not, at least, secure bread and shelter to her child? When she was dead, might not a tie, between the uncle and nephew, be snapped asunder? Would he be as kind to the boy as now when she could commend him with her own lips to his care--when she could place that precious charge into his hands? With these thoughts, she formed one of those resolutions which have all the strength of self-sacrificing love. She would put the boy from her, her last solace and comfort; she would die alone,--alone!

# CHAPTER VIII.

"Constance. When I shall meet him in the court of heaven, I shall not know him."--King John.

One evening, the shop closed and the business done, Mr. Roger Morton and his family sat in that snug and comfortable retreat which generally backs the warerooms of an English tradesman. Happy often, and indeed happy, is that little sanctuary, near to, and yet remote from, the toil and care of the busy mart from which its homely ease and peaceful security are drawn. Glance down those rows of silenced shops in a town at night, and picture the glad and quiet groups gathered within, over that nightly and social meal which custom has banished from the more indolent tribes who neither toil nor spin. Placed between the two extremes of life, the tradesman, who ventures not beyond his means, and sees clear books and sure gains, with enough of occupation to give healthful excitement, enough of fortune to greet each new-born child without a sigh, might be envied alike by those above and those below his state--if the restless heart of men ever envied Content!

"And so the little boy is not to come?" said Mrs. Morton as she crossed her knife and fork, and pushed away her plate, in token that she had done supper.

"I don't know.--Children, go to bed; there--there--that will do. Good night!--Catherine does not say either yes or no. She wants time to consider."

"It was a very handsome offer on our part; some folks never know when they are well off."

"That is very true, my dear, and you are a very sensible person. Kate herself might have been an honest woman, and, what is more, a very rich woman, by this time. She might have married Spencer, the young brewer-- an excellent man, and well to do!"

"Spencer! I don't remember him."

"No: after she went off, he retired from business, and left the place. I don't know what's become of him. He was mightily taken with her, to be sure. She was uncommonly handsome, my sister Catherine."

"Handsome is as handsome does, Mr. Morton," said the wife, who was very much marked with the small-pox. "We all have our temptations and trials; this is a vale of tears, and without grace we are whited sepulchers."

Mr. Morton mixed his brandy and water, and moved his chair into its customary corner.

"You saw your brother's letter," said he, after a pause; "he gives young Philip a very good character."

"The human heart is very deceitful," replied Mrs. Morton, who, by the way, spoke through her nose. "Pray Heaven he may be what he seems; but what's bred in the bone comes out in the flesh."

"We must hope the best," said Mr. Morton, mildly; "and--put another lump into the grog, my dear."

"It is a mercy, I'm thinking, that we didn't have the other little boy. I dare say he has never even been taught his catechism: them people don't know what it is to be a mother. And, besides, it would have been very awkward, Mr. M.; we could never have said who he was: and I've no doubt Miss Pryinall would have been very curious."

"Miss Pryinall be ----!" Mr. Morton checked himself, took a large draught of the brandy and water, and added, "Miss Pryinall wants to have a finger in everybody's pie."

"But she buys a deal of flannel, and does great good to the town; it was she who found out that Mrs. Giles was no better than she should be."

"Poor Mrs. Giles!--she came to the workhouse."

"Poor Mrs. Giles, indeed!  I wonder, Mr. Morton, that you, a married man with a family, should say, poor Mrs. Giles!"

"My dear, when people who have been well off come to the workhouse, they may be called poor:--but that's neither here nor there; only, if the boy does come to us, we must look sharp upon Miss Pryinall."

"I hope he won't come,--it will be very unpleasant.  And when a man has a wife and family, the less he meddles with other folks and their little ones, the better.  For as the Scripture says, 'A man shall cleave to his wife and--'"

Here a sharp, shrill ring at the bell was heard, and Mrs. Morton broke off into:

"Well! I declare! at this hour; who can that be?  And all gone to bed! Do go and see, Mr. Morton."

Somewhat reluctantly and slowly, Mr. Morton rose; and, proceeding to the passage, unbarred the door.  A brief and muttered conversation followed, to the great irritability of Mrs. Morton, who stood in the passage--the candle in her hand.

"What is the matter, Mr. M.?"

Mr. Morton turned back, looking agitated.

"Where's my hat? oh, here.  My sister is come, at the inn."

"Gracious me!  She does not go for to say she is your sister?"

"No, no: here's her note-calls herself a lady that's ill.  I shall be
back soon."

"She can't come here--she sha'n't come here, Mr. M. I'm an honest woman--
she can't come here.  You understand--"

Mr. Morton had naturally a stern countenance, stern to every one but his
wife.  The shrill tone to which he was so long accustomed jarred then on
his heart as well as his ear.  He frowned:

"Pshaw! woman, you have no feeling!" said he, and walked out of the
house, pulling his hat over his brows.  That was the only rude speech Mr.
Morton had ever made to his better half.  She treasured it up in her
heart and memory; it was associated with the sister and the child; and
she was not a woman who ever forgave.

Mr. Morton walked rapidly through the still, moon-lit streets, till he
reached the inn.  A club was held that night in one of the rooms below;
and as he crossed the threshold, the sound of "hip-hip-hurrah!" mingled
with the stamping of feet and the jingling of glasses, saluted his
entrance.  He was a stiff, sober, respectable man,--a man who, except at
elections--he was a great politician--mixed in none of the revels of his
more boisterous townsmen.  The sounds, the spot, were ungenial to him.
He paused, and the colour of shame rose to his brow.  He was ashamed to
be there--ashamed to meet the desolate and, as he believed, erring

sister.

A pretty maidservant, heated and flushed with orders and compliments, crossed his path with a tray full of glasses.

"There's a lady come by the Telegraph?"

"Yes, sir, upstairs, No. 2, Mr. Morton."

Mr. Morton! He shrank at the sound of his own name.

"My wife's right," he muttered. "After all, this is more unpleasant than I thought for."

The slight stairs shook under his hasty tread. He opened the door of No. 2, and that Catherine, whom he had last seen at her age of gay sixteen, radiant with bloom, and, but for her air of pride, the model for a Hebe, --that Catherine, old ere youth was gone, pale, faded, the dark hair silvered over, the cheeks hollow, and the eye dim,--that Catherine fell upon his breast!

"God bless you, brother! How kind to come! How long since we have met!"

"Sit down, Catherine, my dear sister. You are faint--you are very much changed-very. I should not have known you."

"Brother, I have brought my boy; it is painful to part from him--very--very painful: but it is right, and God's will be done." She turned, as she spoke, towards a little, deformed rickety dwarf of a sofa, that seemed to hide itself in the darkest corner of the low, gloomy room; and Morton followed her. With one hand she removed the shawl that she had thrown over the child, and placing the forefinger of the other upon her lips-lips that smiled then--she whispered,--"We will not wake him, he is so tired.  But I would not put him to bed till you had seen him."

And there slept poor Sidney, his fair cheek pillowed on his arm; the soft, silky ringlets thrown from the delicate and unclouded brow; the natural bloom increased by warmth and travel; the lovely face so innocent and hushed; the breathing so gentle and regular, as if never broken by a sigh.

Mr. Morton drew his hand across his eyes.

There was something very touching in the contrast between that wakeful, anxious, forlorn woman, and the slumber of the unconscious boy.  And in that moment, what breast upon which the light of Christian pity--of natural affection, had ever dawned, would, even supposing the world's judgment were true, have recalled Catherine's reputed error?  There is so divine a holiness in the love of a mother, that no matter how the tie that binds her to the child was formed, she becomes, as it were, consecrated and sacred; and the past is forgotten, and the world and its harsh verdicts swept away, when that love alone is visible; and the God, who watches over the little one, sheds His smile over the human deputy, in whose tenderness there breathes His own!

"You will be kind to him--will you not?" said Mrs. Morton; and the appeal was made with that trustful, almost cheerful tone which implies, 'Who would not be kind to a thing so fair and helpless?'  "He is very sensitive and very docile; you will never have occasion to say a hard word to him--never! you have children of your own, brother."

"He is a beautiful boy-beautiful.  I will be a father to him!"

As he spoke,--the recollection of his wife--sour, querulous, austere-- came over him, but he said to himself, "She must take to such a child,-- women always take to beauty."  He bent down and gently pressed his lips

to Sidney's forehead: Mrs. Morton replaced the shawl, and drew her
brother to the other end of the room.

"And now," she said, colouring as she spoke, "I must see your wife,
brother: there is so much to say about a child that only a woman will
recollect. Is she very good-tempered and kind, your wife? You know I
never saw her; you married after--after I left."

"She is a very worthy woman," said Mr. Morton, clearing his throat, "and
brought me some money; she has a will of her own, as most women have; but
that's neither here nor there--she is a good wife as wives go; and
prudent and painstaking--I don't know what I should do without her."

"Brother, I have one favour to request--a great favour."

"Anything I can do in the way of money?"

"It has nothing to do with money. I can't live long--don't shake your
head--I can't live long. I have no fear for Philip, he has so much
spirit--such strength of character--but that child! I cannot bear to
leave him altogether; let me stay in this town--I can lodge anywhere; but
to see him sometimes--to know I shall be in reach if he is ill--let me
stay here--let me die here!"

"You must not talk so sadly--you are young yet--younger than I am--I
don't think of dying."

"Heaven forbid! but--"

"Well--well," interrupted Mr. Morton, who began to fear his feelings
would hurry him into some promise which his wife would not suffer him to
keep; "you shall talk to Margaret,--that is Mrs. Morton--I will get her
to see you--yes, I think I can contrive that; and if you can arrange with

her to stay,--but you see, as she brought the money, and is a very particular woman--"

"I will see her; thank you--thank you; she cannot refuse me."

"And, brother," resumed Mrs. Morton, after a short pause, and speaking in a firm voice--"and is it possible that you disbelieve my story?--that you, like all the rest, consider my children the sons of shame?"

There was an honest earnestness in Catherine's voice, as she spoke, that might have convinced many. But Mr. Morton was a man of facts, a practical man--a man who believed that law was always right, and that the improbable was never true.

He looked down as he answered, "I think you have been a very ill-used woman, Catherine, and that is all I can say on the matter; let us drop the subject."

"No! I was not ill-used; my husband--yes, my husband--was noble and generous from first to last. It was for the sake of his children's prospects--for the expectations they, through him, might derive from his proud uncle--that he concealed our marriage. Do not blame Philip--do not condemn the dead."

"I don't want to blame any one," said Mr. Morton, rather angrily; "I am a plain man--a tradesman, and can only go by what in my class seems fair and honest, which I can't think Mr. Beaufort's conduct was, put it how you will; if he marries you as you think, he gets rid of a witness, he destroys a certificate, and he dies without a will. How ever, all that's neither here nor there. You do quite right not to take the name of Beaufort, since it is an uncommon name, and would always make the story public. Least said, soonest mended. You must always consider that your children will be called natural children, and have their own way to make.

No harm in that! Warm day for your journey." Catherine sighed, and wiped her eyes; she no longer reproached the world, since the son of her own mother disbelieved her.

The relations talked together for some minutes on the past--the present; but there was embarrassment and constraint on both sides--it was so difficult to avoid one subject; and after sixteen years of absence, there is little left in common, even between those who once played together round their parent's knees. Mr. Morton was glad at last to find an excuse in Catherine's fatigue to leave her. "Cheer up, and take a glass of something warm before you go to bed. Good night!" these were his parting words.

Long was the conference, and sleepless the couch, of Mr. and Mrs. Morton. At first that estimable lady positively declared she would not and could not visit Catherine (as to receiving her, that was out of the question). But she secretly resolved to give up that point in order to insist with greater strength upon another-viz., the impossibility of Catherine remaining in the town; such concession for the purpose of resistance being a very common and sagacious policy with married ladies. Accordingly, when suddenly, and with a good grace, Mrs. Morton appeared affected by her husband's eloquence, and said, "Well, poor thing! if she is so ill, and you wish it so much, I will call to-morrow," Mr. Morton felt his heart softened towards the many excellent reasons which his wife urged against allowing Catherine to reside in the town. He was a political character--he had many enemies; the story of his seduced sister, now forgotten, would certainly be raked up; it would affect his comfort, perhaps his trade, certainly his eldest daughter, who was now thirteen; it would be impossible then to adopt the plan hitherto resolved upon--of passing off Sidney as the legitimate orphan of a distant relation; it would be made a great handle for gossip by Miss Pryinall. Added to all these reasons, one not less strong occurred to Mr. Morton himself--the uncommon and merciless rigidity of his wife would render all the other women in the town very glad of any topic that would humble her own sense of immaculate propriety.  Moreover, he saw that if Catherine did remain, it would be a perpetual source of irritation in his own home; he was a man who liked an easy life, and avoided, as far as possible, all food for domestic worry.  And thus, when at length the wedded pair turned back to back, and composed themselves to sleep, the conditions of peace were settled, and the weaker party, as usual in diplomacy, sacrificed to the interests of the united powers.  After breakfast the next morning, Mrs. Morton sallied out on her husband's arm.  Mr. Morton was rather a handsome man, with an air and look grave, composed, severe, that had tended much to raise his character in the town.

Mrs. Morton was short, wiry, and bony.  She had won her husband by making desperate love to him, to say nothing of a dower that enabled him to extend his business, new-front, as well as new-stock his shop, and rise into the very first rank of tradesmen in his native town.  He still believed that she was excessively fond of him--a common delusion of husbands, especially when henpecked.  Mrs. Morton was, perhaps, fond of him in her own way; for though her heart was not warm, there may be a great deal of fondness with very little feeling.  The worthy lady was now clothed in her best.  She had a proper pride in showing the rewards that belong to female virtue.  Flowers adorned her Leghorn bonnet, and her green silk gown boasted four flounces,--such, then, was, I am told, the fashion.  She wore, also, a very handsome black shawl, extremely heavy, though the day was oppressively hot, and with a deep border; a smart *sevigni* brooch of yellow topazes glittered in her breast; a huge gilt serpent glared from her waistband; her hair, or more properly speaking her *front*, was tortured into very tight curls, and her feet into very tight half-laced boots, from which the fragrance of new leather had not yet departed.  It was this last infliction, for il faut souffrir pour etre belle, which somewhat yet more acerbated the ordinary acid of Mrs. Morton's temper.  The sweetest disposition is ruffled when the shoe pinches; and it so happened that Mrs. Roger Morton was one of those ladies who always have chilblains in the winter and corns in the summer. "So you say your sister is a beauty?"

"Was a beauty, Mrs. M.,--was a beauty. People alter."

"A bad conscience, Mr. Morton, is--"

"My dear, can't you walk faster?"

"If you had my corns, Mr. Morton, you would not talk in that way!"

The happy pair sank into silence, only broken by sundry "How d'ye dos?" and "Good mornings!" interchanged with their friends, till they arrived at the inn.

"Let us go up quickly," said Mrs. Morton.

And quiet--quiet to gloom, did the inn, so noisy overnight, seem by morning. The shutters partially closed to keep out the sun--the taproom deserted--the passage smelling of stale smoke--an elderly dog, lazily snapping at the flies, at the foot of the staircase--not a soul to be seen at the bar. The husband and wife, glad to be unobserved, crept on tiptoe up the stairs, and entered Catherine's apartment.

Catherine was seated on the sofa, and Sidney-dressed, like Mrs. Roger Morton, to look his prettiest, nor yet aware of the change that awaited his destiny, but pleased at the excitement of seeing new friends, as handsome children sure of praise and petting usually are--stood by her side.

"My wife--Catherine," said Mr. Morton. Catherine rose eagerly, and gazed searchingly on her sister-in-law's hard face. She swallowed the convulsive rising at her heart as she gazed, and stretched out both her hands, not so much to welcome as to plead. Mrs. Roger Morton drew herself up, and then dropped a courtesy--it was an involuntary piece of good breeding--it was extorted by the noble countenance, the matronly mien of Catherine, different from what she had anticipated--she dropped the courtesy, and Catherine took her hand and pressed it.

"This is my son;" she turned away her head. Sidney advanced towards his protectress who was to be, and Mrs. Roger muttered:

"Come here, my dear! A fine little boy!"

"As fine a child as ever I saw!" said Mr. Morton, heartily, as he took Sidney on his lap, and stroked down his, golden hair.

This displeased Mrs. Roger Morton, but she sat herself down, and said it was "very warm."

"Now go to that lady, my dear," said Mr. Morton. "Is she not a very nice lady?--don't you think you shall like her very much?"

Sidney, the best-mannered child in the world, went boldly up to Mrs. Morton, as he was bid. Mrs. Morton was embarrassed. Some folks are so with other folk's children: a child either removes all constraint from a party, or it increases the constraint tenfold. Mrs. Morton, however, forced a smile, and said, "I have a little boy at home about your age."

"Have you?" exclaimed Catherine, eagerly; and as if that confession made them friends at once, she drew a chair close to her sister-in-law's,--"My brother has told you all?"

"Yes, ma'am."

"And I shall stay here--in the town somewhere--and see him sometimes?"

Mrs. Roger Morton glanced at her husband--her husband glanced at the door--and Catherine's quick eye turned from one to the other.

"Mr. Morton will explain, ma' am," said the wife.

"E-hem!--Catherine, my dear, I am afraid that is out of the question," began Mr. Morton, who, when fairly put to it, could be business-like enough. "You see bygones are bygones, and it is no use raking them up. But many people in the town will recollect you."

"No one will see me--no one, but you and Sidney."

"It will be sure to creep out; won't it, Mrs. Morton?"
"Quite sure. Indeed, ma'am, it is impossible. Mr. Morton is so very respectable, and his neighbours pay so much attention to all he does; and then, if we have an election in the autumn, you see, ma'am, he has a great stake in the place, and is a public character."

"That's neither here nor there," said Mr. Morton. "But I say, Catherine, can your little boy go into the other room for a moment? Margaret, suppose you take him and make friends."

Delighted to throw on her husband the burden of explanation, which she had originally meant to have all the importance of giving herself in her most proper and patronising manner, Mrs. Morton twisted her fingers into the boy's hand, and, opening the door that communicated with the bedroom, left the brother and sister alone. And then Mr. Morton, with more tact and delicacy than might have been expected from him, began to soften to Catherine the hard ship of the separation he urged. He dwelt principally on what was best for the child. Boys were so brutal in their intercourse with each other. He had even thought it better represent Philip to Mr. Plaskwith as a more distant relation than he was; and he begged, by the by, that Catherine would tell Philip to take the hint. But as for Sidney, sooner or later, he would go to a day-school--have companions of his own age--if his birth were known, he would be exposed to many mortifications--so much better, and so very easy, to bring him up as the lawful, that is the legal, offspring of some distant relation.

"And," cried poor Catherine, clasping her bands, "when I am dead, is he never to know that I was his mother?" The anguish of that question thrilled the heart of the listener. He was affected below all the surface that worldly thoughts and habits had laid, stratum by stratum, over the humanities within. He threw his arms round Catherine, and strained her to his breast:

"No, my sister--my poor sister-he shall know it when he is old enough to understand, and to keep his own secret. He shall know, too, how we all loved and prized you once; how young you were, how flattered and tempted; how you were deceived, for I know that--on my soul I do--I know it was not your fault. He shall know, too, how fondly you loved your child, and how you sacrificed, for his sake, the very comfort of being near him. He shall know it all--all--"

"My brother--my brother, I resign him--I am content. God reward you. I will go--go quickly. I know you will take care of him now."

"And you see," resumed Mr. Morton, re-settling himself, and wiping his eyes, "it is best, between you and me, that Mrs. Morton should have her own way in this. She is a very good woman--very; but it's prudent not to vex her. You may come in now, Mrs. Morton."

Mrs. Morton and Sidney reappeared.

"We have settled it all," said the husband. "When can we have him?"

"Not to-day," said Mrs. Roger Morton; "you see, ma'am, we must get his bed ready, and his sheets well aired: I am very particular."

"Certainly, certainly.  Will he sleep alone?--pardon me."

"He shall have a room to himself," said Mr. Morton.  "Eh, my dear?  Next to Martha's.  Martha is our parlourmaid--very good-natured girl, and fond of children."

Mrs. Morton looked grave, thought a moment, and said, "Yes, he can have that room."

"Who can have that room?" asked Sidney, innocently.  "You, my dear," replied Mr. Morton.

"And where will mamma sleep?  I must sleep near mamma."

"Mamma is going away," said Catherine, in a firm voice, in which the despair would only have been felt by the acute ear of sympathy,--"going away for a little time: but this gentleman and lady will be very--very kind to you."

"We will do our best, ma'am," said Mrs. Morton.

And as she spoke, a sudden light broke on the boy's mind--he uttered a loud cry, broke from his aunt, rushed to his mother's breast, and hid his face there, sobbing bitterly.

"I am afraid he has been very much spoiled," whispered Mrs. Roger Morton.  "I don't think we need stay longer--it will look suspicious.  Good morning, ma'am: we shall be ready to-morrow."

"Good-bye, Catherine," said Mr. Morton; and he added, as he kissed her,

"Be of good heart, I will come up by myself and spend the evening with you."

It was the night after this interview. Sidney had gone to his new home; they had been all kind to him--Mr. Morton, the children, Martha the parlour-maid. Mrs. Roger herself had given him a large slice of bread and jam, but had looked gloomy all the rest of the evening: because, like a dog in a strange place, he refused to eat. His little heart was full, and his eyes, swimming with tears, were turned at every moment to the door. But he did not show the violent grief that might have been expected. His very desolation, amidst the unfamiliar faces, awed and chilled him. But when Martha took him to bed, and undressed him, and he knelt down to say his prayers, and came to the words, "Pray God bless dear mamma, and make me a good child," his heart could contain its load no longer, and he sobbed with a passion that alarmed the good-natured servant. She had been used, however, to children, and she soothed and caressed him, and told him of all the nice things he would do, and the nice toys he would have; and at last, silenced, if not convinced, his eyes closed, and, the tears yet wet on their lashes, he fell asleep.

It had been arranged that Catherine should return home that night by a late coach, which left the town at twelve. It was already past eleven. Mrs. Morton had retired to bed; and her husband, who had, according to his wont, lingered behind to smoke a cigar over his last glass of brandy and water, had just thrown aside the stump, and was winding up his watch, when he heard a low tap at his window. He stood mute and alarmed, for the window opened on a back lane, dark and solitary at night, and, from the heat of the weather, the iron-cased shutter was not yet closed; the sound was repeated, and he heard a faint voice. He glanced at the poker, and then cautiously moved to the window, and looked forth,--"Who's there?"

"It is I--it is Catherine! I cannot go without seeing my boy. I must see him--I must, once more!"

"My dear sister, the place is shut up--it is impossible. God bless me, if Mrs. Morton should hear you!"

"I have walked before this window for hours--I have waited till all is hushed in your house, till no one, not even a menial, need see the mother stealing to the bed of her child. Brother, by the memory of our own mother, I command you to let me look, for the last time, upon my boy's face!"

As Catherine said this, standing in that lonely street--darkness and solitude below, God and the stars above--there was about her a majesty which awed the listener. Though she was so near, her features were not very clearly visible; but her attitude--her hand raised aloft--the outline of her wasted but still commanding form, were more impressive from the shadowy dimness of the air.

"Come round, Catherine," said Mr. Morton after a pause; "I will admit you."

He shut the window, stole to the door, unbarred it gently, and admitted his visitor. He bade her follow him; and, shading the light with his hand, crept up the stairs. Catherine's step made no sound.

They passed, unmolested, and unheard, the room in which the wife was drowsily reading, according to her custom before she tied her nightcap and got into bed, a chapter in some pious book. They ascended to the chamber where Sidney lay; Morton opened the door cautiously, and stood at the threshold, so holding the candle that its light might not wake the child, though it sufficed to guide Catherine to the bed. The room was small, perhaps close, but scrupulously clean; for cleanliness was Mrs. Roger Morton's capital virtue. The mother, with a tremulous hand, drew aside the white curtains, and checked her sobs as she gazed on the young quiet face that was turned towards her. She gazed some moments in passionate silence; who shall say, beneath that silence, what thoughts, what prayers moved and stirred!

Then bending down, with pale, convulsive lips she kissed the little hands thrown so listlessly on the coverlet of the pillow on which the head lay. After this she turned her face to her brother with a mute appeal in her glance, took a ring from her finger--a ring that had never till then left it--the ring which Philip Beaufort had placed there the day after that child was born. "Let him wear this round his neck," said she, and stopped, lest she should sob aloud, and disturb the boy. In that gift she felt as if she invoked the father's spirit to watch over the friendless orphan; and then, pressing together her own hands firmly, as we do in some paroxysm of great pain, she turned from the room, descended the stairs, gained the street, and muttered to her brother, "I am happy now; peace be on these thresholds!" Before he could answer she was gone.

# CHAPTER IX.

"Thus things are strangely wrought,
While joyful May doth last;
Take May in Time--when May is gone
The pleasant time is past."--RICHARD EDWARDS.
From the Paradise of Dainty Devices.

It was that period of the year when, to those who look on the surface of society, London wears its most radiant smile; when shops are gayest, and trade most brisk; when down the thoroughfares roll and glitter the countless streams of indolent and voluptuous life; when the upper class spend, and the middle class make; when the ball-room is the Market of Beauty, and the club-house the School for Scandal; when the hells yawn for their prey, and opera-singers and fiddlers--creatures hatched from gold, as the dung-flies from the dung-swarm, and buzz, and fatten, round the hide of the gentle Public  In the cant phase, it was "the London season."  And happy, take it altogether, happy above the rest of the year, even for the hapless, is that period of ferment and fever.  It is not the season for duns, and the debtor glides about with a less anxious eye; and the weather is warm, and the vagrant sleeps, unfrozen, under the starlit portico; and the beggar thrives, and the thief rejoices--for the rankness of the civilisation has superfluities clutched by all.  And out of the general corruption things sordid and things miserable crawl forth to bask in the common sunshine--things that perish when the first autumn winds whistle along the melancholy city.  It is the gay time for the heir and the beauty, and the statesman and the lawyer, and the mother with her young daughters, and the artist with his fresh pictures, and the poet with his new book.  It is the gay time, too, for the starved journeyman, and the ragged outcast that with long stride and patient eyes follows, for pence, the equestrian, who bids him go and be d---d in vain.  It is a gay time for the painted harlot in a crimson pelisse; and a gay time for the old hag that loiters about the thresholds of the gin-shop, to buy back, in a draught, the dreams of departed youth.  It is gay, in fine, as the fulness of a vast city is ever gay--for Vice as for Innocence, for Poverty as for Wealth.  And the wheels of every single destiny wheel on the merrier, no matter whether they are bound to Heaven or to Hell.

Arthur Beaufort, the young heir, was at his father's house.  He was fresh from Oxford, where he had already discovered that learning is not better than house and land.  Since the new prospects opened to him, Arthur Beaufort was greatly changed.  Naturally studious and prudent, had his fortunes remained what they had been before his uncle's death, he would probably have become a laborious and distinguished man.  But though his abilities were good, he had not those restless impulses which belong to

Genius--often not only its glory, but its curse. The Golden Rod cast his
energies asleep at once. Good-natured to a fault, and somewhat
vacillating in character, he adopted the manner and the code of the rich
young idlers who were his equals at College. He became, like them,
careless, extravagant, and fond of pleasure. This change, if it
deteriorated his mind, improved his exterior. It was a change that
could not but please women; and of all women his mother the most. Mrs.
Beaufort was a lady of high birth; and in marrying her, Robert had hoped
much from the interest of her connections; but a change in the ministry
had thrown her relations out of power; and, beyond her dowry, he obtained
no worldly advantage with the lady of his mercenary choice. Mrs.
Beaufort was a woman whom a word or two will describe. She was
thoroughly commonplace--neither bad nor good, neither clever nor silly.
She was what is called well-bred; that is, languid, silent, perfectly
dressed, and insipid. Of her two children, Arthur was almost the
exclusive favourite, especially after he became the heir to such
brilliant fortunes. For she was so much the mechanical creature of the
world, that even her affection was warm or cold in proportion as the
world shone on it. Without being absolutely in love with her husband,
she liked him--they suited each other; and (in spite of all the
temptations that had beset her in their earlier years, for she had been
esteemed a beauty--and lived, as worldly people must do, in circles where
examples of unpunished gallantry are numerous and contagious) her conduct
had ever been scrupulously correct. She had little or no feeling for
misfortunes with which she had never come into contact; for those with
which she had--such as the distresses of younger sons, or the errors of
fashionable women, or the disappointments of "a proper ambition"--she had
more sympathy than might have been supposed, and touched on them with all
the tact of well-bred charity and ladylike forbearance. Thus, though she
was regarded as a strict person in point of moral decorum, yet in society
she was popular-as women at once pretty and inoffensive generally are.

To do Mrs. Beaufort justice, she had not been privy to the letter her husband wrote to Catherine, although not wholly innocent of it. The fact is, that Robert had never mentioned to her the peculiar circumstances that made Catherine an exception from ordinary rules--the generous propositions of his brother to him the night before his death; and, whatever his incredulity as to the alleged private marriage, the perfect loyalty and faith that Catherine had borne to the deceased,--he had merely observed, "I must do something, I suppose, for that woman; she very nearly entrapped my poor brother into marrying her; and he would then, for what I know, have cut Arthur out of the estates. Still, I must do something for her--eh?"

"Yes, I think so. What was she?-very low?"

"A tradesman's daughter."

"The children should be provided for according to the rank of the mother; that's the general rule in such cases: and the mother should have about the same provision she might have looked for if she had married a tradesman and been left a widow. I dare say she was a very artful kind of person, and don't deserve anything; but it is always handsomer, in the eyes of the world, to go by the general rules people lay down as to money matters."

So spoke Mrs. Beaufort. She concluded her husband had settled the matter, and never again recurred to it. Indeed, she had never liked the late Mr. Beaufort, whom she considered *mauvais ton*.

In the breakfast-room at Mr. Beaufort's, the mother and son were seated; the former at work, the latter lounging by the window: they were not alone. In a large elbow-chair sat a middle-aged man, listening, or appearing to listen, to the prattle of a beautiful little girl--Arthur Beaufort's sister. This man was not handsome, but there was a certain elegance in his air, and a certain intelligence in his countenance, which made his appearance pleasing. He had that kind of eye which is often seen with red hair--an eye of a reddish hazel, with very long lashes; the eyebrows were dark, and clearly defined; and the short hair showed to advantage the contour of a small well-shaped head. His features were irregular; the complexion had been sanguine, but was now faded, and a yellow tinge mingled with the red. His face was more wrinkled, especially round the eyes--which, when he laughed, were scarcely visible --than is usual even in men ten years older. But his teeth were still of a dazzling whiteness; nor was there any trace of decayed health in his countenance. He seemed one who had lived hard; but who had much yet left in the lamp wherewith to feed the wick. At the first glance he appeared slight, as he lolled listlessly in his chair--almost fragile. But, at a nearer examination, you perceived that, in spite of the small extremities and delicate bones, his frame was constitutionally strong. Without being broad in the shoulders, he was exceedingly deep in the chest--deeper than men who seemed giants by his side; and his gestures had the ease of one accustomed to an active life. He had, indeed, been celebrated in his youth for his skill in athletic exercises, but a wound, received in a duel many years ago, had rendered him lame for life--a misfortune which interfered with his former habits, and was said to have soured his temper. This personage, whose position and character will be described hereafter, was Lord Lilburne, the brother of Mrs. Beaufort.

"So, Camilla," said Lord Lilburne to his niece, as carelessly, not fondly, he stroked down her glossy ringlets, "you don't like Berkeley Square as you did Gloucester Place."

"Oh, no! not half so much! You see I never walk out in the fields, --[Now the Regent's Park.]--nor make daisy-chains at Primrose Hill. I don't know what mamma means," added the child, in a whisper, "in saying we are better off here."

Lord Lilburne smiled, but the smile was a half sneer. "You will know quite soon enough, Camilla; the understandings of young ladies grow up very quickly on this side of Oxford Street.  Well, Arthur, and what are your plans to-day?"

"Why," said Arthur, suppressing a yawn, "I have promised to ride out with a friend of mine, to see a horse that is for sale somewhere in the suburbs."

As he spoke, Arthur rose, stretched himself, looked in the glass, and then glanced impatiently at the window.

"He ought to be here by this time."

"He! who?"  said Lord Lilburne, "the horse or the other animal--I mean the friend?"

"The friend," answered Arthur, smiling, but colouring while he smiled, for he half suspected the quiet sneer of his uncle.

"Who is your friend, Arthur?" asked Mrs. Beaufort, looking up from her work.

"Watson, an Oxford man.  By the by, I must introduce him to you."

"Watson! what Watson? what family of Watson?  Some Watsons are good and some are bad," said Mrs. Beaufort, musingly.

"Then they are very unlike the rest of mankind," observed Lord Lilburne, drily.

"Oh! my Watson is a very gentlemanlike person, I assure you," said Arthur, half-laughing, "and you need not be ashamed of him."  Then, rather desirous of turning the conversation, he continued, "So my father will be back from Beaufort Court to-day?"

"Yes; he writes in excellent spirits. He says the rents will bear raising at least ten per cent., and that the house will not require much repair."

Here Arthur threw open the window.

"Ah, Watson! how are you? How d'ye do, Marsden? Danvers, too! that's capital! the more the merrier! I will be down in an instant. But would you not rather come in?"

"An agreeable inundation," murmured Lord Lilburne. "Three at a time: he takes your house for Trinity College."

A loud, clear voice, however, declined the invitation; the horses were heard pawing without. Arthur seized his hat and whip, and glanced to his mother and uncle, smilingly. "Good-bye! I shall be out till dinner. Kiss me, my pretty Milly!" And as his sister, who had run to the window, sickening for the fresh air and exercise he was about to enjoy, now turned to him wistful and mournful eyes, the kind-hearted young man took her in his arms, and whispered while he kissed her:

"Get up early to-morrow, and we'll have such a nice walk together."

Arthur was gone: his mother's gaze had followed his young and graceful figure to the door.

"Own that he is handsome, Lilburne. May I not say more:--has he not the proper air?"

"My dear sister, your son will be rich. As for his air, he has plenty of airs, but wants graces."

"Then who could polish him like yourself?"

"Probably no one.  But had I a son--which Heaven forbid!--he should not have me for his Mentor.  Place a young man--(go and shut the door, Camilla!)--between two vices--women and gambling, if you want to polish him into the fashionable smoothness. *Entre nous*, the varnish is a little expensive!"

Mrs. Beaufort sighed.  Lord Lilburne smiled.  He had a strange pleasure in hurting the feelings of others.  Besides, he disliked youth: in his own youth he had enjoyed so much that he grew sour when he saw the young.

Meanwhile Arthur Beaufort and his friends, careless of the warmth of the day, were laughing merrily, and talking gaily, as they made for the suburb of H----.

"It is an out-of-the-way place for a horse, too," said Sir Harry Danvers.

"But I assure you," insisted Mr. Watson, earnestly, that my groom, who is a capital judge, says it is the cleverest hack he ever mounted.  It has won several trotting matches.  It belonged to a sporting tradesman, now done up.  The advertisement caught me."

"Well," said Arthur, gaily, "at all events the ride is delightful.  What weather!  You must all dine with me at Richmond to-morrow--we will row back."

"And a little chicken-hazard, at the M---, afterwards," said Mr. Marsden, who was an elder, not a better, man than the rest--a handsome, saturnine man--who had just left Oxford, and was already known on the turf.

"Anything you please," said Arthur, making his horse curvet.

Oh, Mr. Robert Beaufort! Mr. Robert Beaufort! could your prudent, scheming, worldly heart but feel what devil's tricks your wealth was playing with a son who if poor had been the pride of the Beauforts! On one side of our pieces of old we see the saint trampling down the dragon. False emblem! Reverse it on the coin! In the real use of the gold, it is the dragon who tramples down the saint! But on--on! the day is bright and your companions merry; make the best of your green years, Arthur Beaufort!

The young men had just entered the suburb of H---, and were spurring on four abreast at a canter. At that time an old man, feeling his way before him with a stick,--for though not quite blind, he saw imperfectly,--was crossing the road. Arthur and his friends, in loud converse, did not observe the poor passenger. He stopped abruptly, for his ear caught the sound of danger--it was too late: Mr. Marsden's horse, hard-mouthed, and high-stepping, came full against him. Mr. Marsden looked down:

"Hang these old men! always in the way," said he, plaintively, and in the tone of a much-injured person, and, with that, Mr. Marsden rode on. But the others, who were younger--who were not gamblers--who were not yet grinded down into stone by the world's wheels--the others halted. Arthur Beaufort leaped from his horse, and the old man was already in his arms; but he was severely hurt. The blood trickled from his forehead; he complained of pains in his side and limbs.

"Lean on me, my poor fellow! Do you live far off? I will take you home."

"Not many yards. This would not have happened if I had had my dog. Never mind, sir, go your way. It is only an old man--what of that? I wish I had my dog."

"I will join you," said Arthur to his friends; "my groom has the direction. I will just take the poor old man home, and send for a surgeon. I shall not be long."

"So like you, Beaufort: the best fellow in the world!" said Mr. Watson, with some emotion. "And there's Marsden positively, dismounted, and looking at his horse's knees as if they could be hurt! Here's a sovereign for you, my man."

"And here's another," said Sir Harry; "so that's settled. Well, you will join us, Beaufort? You see the yard yonder. We'll wait twenty minutes for you. Come on, Watson." The old man had not picked up the sovereigns thrown at his feet, neither had he thanked the donors. And on his countenance there was a sour, querulous, resentful expression.

"Must a man be a beggar because he is run over, or because he is half blind?" said he, turning his dim, wandering eyes painfully towards Arthur. "Well, I wish I had my dog!"

"I will supply his place," said Arthur, soothingly. "Come, lean on me--heavier; that's right. You are not so bad,--eh?"

"Um!--the sovereigns!--it is wicked to leave them in the kennel!"

Arthur smiled. "Here they are, sir."

The old man slid the coins into his pocket, and Arthur continued to talk, though he got but short answers, and those only in the way of direction, till at last the old man stopped at the door of a small house near the churchyard.

After twice ringing the bell, the door was opened by a middle-aged woman, whose appearance was above that of a common menial; dressed, somewhat gaily for her years, in a cap seated very far back on a black ***touroet***, and decorated with red ribands, an apron made out of an Indian silk handkerchief, a puce-coloured sarcenet gown, black silk stockings, long gilt earrings, and a watch at her girdle.

"Bless us and save us, sir! What has happened?" exclaimed this worthy personage, holding up her hands.

"Pish! I am faint: let me in. I don't want your aid any more, sir. Thank you. Good day!"

Not discouraged by this farewell, the churlish tone of which fell harmless on the invincibly sweet temper of Arthur, the young man continued to assist the sufferer along the narrow passage into a little old-fashioned parlour; and no sooner was the owner deposited on his worm-eaten leather chair than he fainted away. On reaching the house, Arthur had sent his servant (who had followed him with the horses) for the nearest surgeon; and while the woman was still employed, after taking off the sufferer's cravat, in burning feathers under his nose, there was heard a sharp rap and a shrill ring. Arthur opened the door, and admitted a smart little man in nankeen breeches and gaiters. He bustled into the room.

"What's this--bad accident--um--um! Sad thing, very sad. Open the window. A glass of water--a towel."

"So--so: I see--I see--no fracture--contusion. Help him off with his coat. Another chair, ma'am; put up his poor legs. What age is he, ma'am?--Sixty-eight! Too old to bleed. Thank you. How is it, sir? Poorly, to be sure will be comfortable presently--faintish still? Soon put all to rights."

"Tray! Tray! Where's my dog, Mrs. Boxer?"

"Lord, sir, what do you want with your dog now? He is in the back-yard."

"And what business has my dog in the back-yard?" almost screamed the sufferer, in accents that denoted no diminution of vigour. "I thought as soon as my back was turned my dog would be ill-used! Why did I go without my dog? Let in my dog directly, Mrs. Boxer!"

"All right, you see, sir," said the apothecary, turning to Beaufort-- "no cause for alarm--very comforting that little passion--does him good-- sets one's mind easy. How did it happen? Ah, I understand! knocked down--might have been worse. Your groom (sharp fellow!) explained in a trice, sir. Thought it was my old friend here by the description. Worthy man--settled here a many year--very odd-eccentric (this in a whisper). Came off instantly: just at dinner--cold lamb and salad. 'Mrs. Perkins,' says I, 'if any one calls for me, I shall be at No. 4, Prospect Place.' Your servant observed the address, sir. Oh, very sharp fellow! See how the old gentleman takes to his dog--fine little dog--what a stump of a tail! Deal of practice--expect two accouchements every hour. Hot weather for childbirth. So says I to Mrs. Perkins, 'If Mrs. Plummer is taken, or Mrs. Everat, or if old Mr. Grub has another fit, send off at once to No. 4. Medical men should be always in the way-- that's my maxim. Now, sir, where do you feel the pain?"

"In my ears, sir."

"Bless me, that looks bad. How long have you felt it?"

"Ever since you have been in the room."

"Oh! I take. Ha! ha!--very eccentric--very!" muttered the apothecary, a little disconcerted. "Well, let him lie down, ma'am. I'll send him a little quieting draught to be taken directly--pill at night, aperient in the morning. If wanted, send for me--always to be found. Bless me, that's my boy Bob's ring. Please to open the door, ma' am. Know his ring--very peculiar knack of his own. Lay ten to one it is Mrs. Plummer, or perhaps. Mrs. Everat--her ninth child in eight years--in the grocery line. A woman in a thousand, sir!"

Here a thin boy, with very short coat-sleeves, and very large hands, burst into the room with his mouth open. "Sir--Mr. Perkins--sir!"

"I know--I know-coming. Mrs. Plummer or Mrs. Everat?"

"No, sir; it be the poor lady at Mrs. Lacy's; she be taken desperate. Mrs. Lacy's girl has just been over to the shop, and made me run here to you, sir."

"Mrs. Lacy's! oh, I know. Poor Mrs. Morton! Bad case--very bad--must be off. Keep him quiet, ma'am. Good day! Look in to-morrow-nine o'clock. Put a little lint with the lotion on the head, ma'am. Mrs. Morton! Ah! bad job that."

Here the apothecary had shuffled himself off to the street door, when Arthur laid his hand on his arm.

"Mrs. Morton! Did you say Morton, sir? What kind of a person--is she very ill?"

"Hopeless case, sir--general break-up. Nice woman--quite the lady--known better days, I'm sure."

"Has she any children--sons?"

"Two--both away now--fine lads--quite wrapped up in them--youngest especially."

"Good heavens! it must be she--ill, and dying, and destitute, perhaps,"-- exclaimed Arthur, with real and deep feeling; "I will go with you, sir. I fancy that I know this lady--that," he added generously, "I am related to her."

"Do you?--glad to hear it. Come along, then; she ought to have some one near her besides servants: not but what Jenny, the maid, is uncommonly kind. Dr. -----, who attends her sometimes, said to me, says he, 'It is the mind, Mr. Perkins; I wish we could get back her boys."

"And where are they?"

"'Prenticed out, I fancy. Master Sidney--"

"Sidney!"

"Ah! that was his name--pretty name. D'ye know Sir Sidney Smith?-- extraordinary man, sir! Master Sidney was a beautiful child--quite spoiled. She always fancied him ailing--always sending for me. 'Mr. Perkins,' said she, 'there's something the matter with my child; I'm sure there is, though he won't own it. He has lost his appetite--had a headache last night.' 'Nothing the matter, ma'am,' says I; 'wish you'd think more of yourself.'

"These mothers are silly, anxious, poor creatures. Nater, sir, Nater-- wonderful thing--Nater!--Here we are."

And the apothecary knocked at the private door of a milliner and hosier's shop.

# CHAPTER X.

"Thy child shall live, and I will see it nourished."--Titus Andronicus.

As might be expected, the excitement and fatigue of Catherine's journey to N---- had considerably accelerated the progress of disease. And when she reached home, and looked round the cheerless rooms all solitary, all hushed--Sidney gone, gone from her for ever, she felt, indeed, as if the last reed on which she had leaned was broken, and her business upon earth was done. Catherine was not condemned to absolute poverty--the poverty which grinds and gnaws, the poverty of rags and famine. She had still left nearly half of such portion of the little capital, realised by the sale of her trinkets, as had escaped the clutch of the law; and her brother had forced into her hands a note for L20. with an assurance that the same sum should be paid to her half-yearly. Alas! there was little chance of her needing it again! She was not, then, in want of means to procure the common comforts of life. But now a new passion had entered into her breast--the passion of the miser; she wished to hoard every sixpence as some little provision for her children. What was the use of her feeding a lamp nearly extinguished, and which was fated to be soon broken up and cast amidst the vast lumber-house of Death? She would willingly have removed into a more homely lodging, but the servant of the house had been so fond of Sidney--so kind to him. She clung to one familiar face on which there seemed to live the reflection of her child's. But she relinquished the first floor for the second; and there, day by day, she felt her eyes grow heavier and heavier beneath the clouds of the last sleep. Besides the aid of Mr. Perkins, a kind enough man in his way, the good physician whom she had before consulted, still attended her, and refused his fee. Shocked at perceiving that she rejected every little alleviation of her condition, and wishing at least to procure for her last hours the society of one of her sons, he had inquired the address of the elder; and on the day preceding the one in which Arthur discovered her abode, he despatched to Philip the following letter:

"SIR:--Being called in to attend your mother in a lingering illness, which I fear may prove fatal, I think it my duty to request you to come to her as soon as you receive this. Your presence cannot but be a great comfort to her. The nature of her illness is such that it is impossible to calculate exactly how long she may be spared to you; but I am sure her fate might be prolonged, and her remaining days more happy, if she could be induced to remove into a better air and a more quiet neighbourhood, to take more generous sustenance, and, above all, if her mind could be set more at ease as to your and your brother's prospects. You must pardon me if I have seemed inquisitive; but I have sought to draw from your mother some particulars as to her family and connections, with a wish to represent to them her state of mind. She is, however, very reserved on these points. If, however, you have relations well to do in the world, I think some application to them should be made. I fear the state of her affairs weighs much upon your poor mother's mind; and I must leave you to judge how far it can be relieved by the good feeling of any persons upon whom she may have legitimate claims. At all events, I repeat my wish that you should come to her forthwith.

"I am, &c."

After the physician had despatched this letter, a sudden and marked alteration for the worse took place in his patient's disorder; and in the visit he had paid that morning, he saw cause to fear that her hours on earth would be much fewer than he had before anticipated. He had left her, however, comparatively better; but two hours after his departure, the symptoms of her disease had become very alarming, and the good-natured servant girl, her sole nurse, and who had, moreover, the whole business of the other lodgers to attend to, had, as we have seen, thought it necessary to summon the apothecary in the interval that must elapse before she could reach the distant part of the metropolis in which Dr. ---- resided.

On entering the chamber, Arthur felt all the remorse, which of right belonged to his father, press heavily on his soul. What a contrast, that mean and solitary chamber, and its comfortless appurtenances, to the graceful and luxurious abode where, full of health and hope, he had last beheld her, the mother of Philip Beaufort's children! He remained silent till Mr. Perkins, after a few questions, retired to send his drugs. He then approached the bed; Catherine, though very weak and suffering much pain, was still sensible. She turned her dim eyes on the young man; but she did not recognise his features.

"You do not remember me?" said he, in a voice struggling with tears: "I am Arthur--Arthur Beaufort." Catherine made no answer.

"Good Heavens! Why do I see you here? I believed you with your friends --your children provided for--as became my father to do. He assured me that you were so." Still no answer.

And then the young man, overpowered with the feelings of a sympathising and generous nature, forgetting for a while Catherine's weakness, poured forth a torrent of inquiries, regrets, and self-upbraidings, which Catherine at first little heeded. But the name of her children, repeated again and again, struck upon that chord which, in a woman's heart, is the last to break; and she raised herself in her bed, and looked at her visitor wistfully.

"Your father," she said, then--"your father was unlike my Philip; but I see things differently now. For me, all bounty is too late; but my children--to-morrow they may have no mother. The law is with you, but not justice! You will be rich and powerful;--will you befriend my children?"

"Through life, so help me Heaven!" exclaimed Arthur, falling on his knees beside the bed.

What then passed between them it is needless to detail; for it was little, save broken repetitions of the same prayer and the same response. But there was so much truth and earnestness in Arthur's voice and countenance, that Catherine felt as if an angel had come there to administer comfort. And when late in the day the physician entered, he found his patient leaning on the breast of her young visitor, and looking on his face with a happy smile.

The physician gathered enough from the appearance of Arthur and the gossip of Mr. Perkins, to conjecture that one of the rich relations he had attributed to Catherine was arrived. Alas! for her it was now indeed too late!

# CHAPTER XI.

"D'ye stand amazed?--Look o'er thy head, Maximinian!
Look to the terror which overhangs thee."
BEAUMONT AND FLETCHER: *The Prophetess*.

Phillip had been five weeks in his new home: in another week, he was to enter on his articles of apprenticeship. With a stern, unbending gloom of manner, he had commenced the duties of his novitiate. He submitted to all that was enjoined him. He seemed to have lost for ever the wild and unruly waywardness that had stamped his boyhood; but he was never seen to smile--he scarcely ever opened his lips. His very soul seemed to have quitted him with its faults; and he performed all the functions of his situation with the quiet listless regularity of a machine. Only when the work was done and the shop closed, instead of joining the family circle in the back parlour, he would stroll out in the dusk of the evening, away from the town, and not return till the hour at which the family retired to rest. Punctual in all he did, he never exceeded that hour. He had heard once a week from his mother; and only on the mornings in which he expected a letter, did he seem restless and agitated. Till the postman entered the shop, he was as pale as death--his hands trembling--his lips compressed. When he read the letter he became composed for Catherine sedulously concealed from her son the state of her health: she wrote cheerfully, besought him to content himself with the state into which he had fallen, and expressed her joy that in his letters he intimated that content; for the poor boy's letters were not less considerate than her own. On her return from her brother, she had so far silenced or concealed her misgivings as to express satisfaction at the home she had provided for Sidney; and she even held out hopes of some future when, their probation finished and their independence secured, she might reside with her sons alternately. These hopes redoubled Philip's assiduity, and he saved every shilling of his weekly stipend; and sighed as he thought that in another week his term of apprenticeship would commence, and the stipend cease.

Mr. Plaskwith could not but be pleased on the whole with the diligence of his assistant, but he was chafed and irritated by the sullenness of his manner. As for Mrs. Plaskwith, poor woman! she positively detested the taciturn and moody boy, who never mingled in the jokes of the circle, nor played with the children, nor complimented her, nor added, in short, anything to the sociability of the house. Mr. Plimmins, who had at first sought to condescend, next sought to bully; but the gaunt frame and savage eye of Philip awed the smirk youth, in spite of himself; and he confessed to Mrs. Plaskwith that he should not like to meet "the gipsy," alone, on a dark night; to which Mrs. Plaskwith replied, as usual, "that Mr. Plimmins always did say the best things in the world!"

One morning, Philip was sent a few miles into the country, to assist in cataloguing some books in the library of Sir Thomas Champerdown--that gentleman, who was a scholar, having requested that some one acquainted with the Greek character might be sent to him, and Philip being the only one in the shop who possessed such knowledge.

It was evening before he returned.  Mr. and Mrs. Plaskwith were both in the shop as he entered--in fact, they had been employed in talking him over.

"I can't abide him!" cried Mrs. Plaskwith.  "If you choose to take him for good, I sha'n't have an easy moment.  I'm sure the 'prentice that cut his master's throat at Chatham, last week, was just like him."

"Pshaw! Mrs. P.," said the bookseller, taking a huge pinch of snuff, as usual, from his waistcoat pocket.  "I myself was reserved when I was young; all reflective people are.  I may observe, by the by, that it was the case with Napoleon Buonaparte: still, however, I must own he is a disagreeable youth, though he attends to his business."

"And how fond of money he is!" remarked Mrs. Plaskwith, "he won't buy himself a new pair of shoes!--quite disgraceful!  And did you see what a look he gave Plimmins, when he joked about his indifference to his sole?  Plimmins always does say such good things!"

"He is shabby, certainly," said the bookseller; "but the value of a book does not always depend on the binding."

"I hope he is honest!" observed Mrs. Plaskwith;--and here Philip entered.

"Hum," said Mr. Plaskwith; "you have had a long day's work: but I suppose it will take a week to finish?"

"I am to go again to-morrow morning, sir: two days more will conclude the task."

"There's a letter for you," cried Mrs. Plaskwith; "you owes me for it."

"A letter!" It was not his mother's hand--it was a strange writing--he gasped for breath as he broke the seal. It was the letter of the physician.

His mother, then, was ill-dying-wanting, perhaps, the necessaries of life. She would have concealed from him her illness and her poverty. His quick alarm exaggerated the last into utter want;--he uttered a cry that rang through the shop, and rushed to Mr. Plaskwith.

"Sir, sir! my mother is dying! She is poor, poor, perhaps starving;-- money, money!--lend me money!--ten pounds!--five!--I will work for you all my life for nothing, but lend me the money!"

"Hoity-toity!" said Mrs. Plaskwith, nudging her husband--"I told you what would come of it: it will be 'money or life' next time."

Philip did not heed or hear this address; but stood immediately before the bookseller, his hands clasped--wild impatience in his eyes. Mr. Plaskwith, somewhat stupefied, remained silent.

"Do you hear me?--are you human?" exclaimed Philip, his emotion revealing at once all the fire of his character. "I tell you my mother is dying; I must go to her! Shall I go empty-handed! Give me money!"

Mr. Plaskwith was not a bad-hearted man; but he was a formal man, and an irritable one. The tone his shopboy (for so he considered Philip) assumed to him, before his own wife too (examples are very dangerous), rather exasperated than moved him.

"That's not the way to speak to your master:--you forget yourself, young man!"

"Forget!--But, sir, if she has not necessaries-if she is starving?"

"Fudge!" said Plaskwith. "Mr. Morton writes me word that he has provided for your mother! Does he not, Hannah?"

"More fool he, I'm sure, with such a fine family of his own! Don't look at me in that way, young man; I won't take it--that I won't! I declare my blood friz to see you!"

"Will you advance me money?--five pounds--only five pounds, Mr. Plaskwith?"

"Not five shillings! Talk to me in this style!--not the man for it, sir!--highly improper. Come, shut up the shop, and recollect yourself; and, perhaps, when Sir Thomas's library is done, I may let you go to town. You can't go to-morrow. All a sham, perhaps; eh, Hannah?"

"Very likely! Consult Plimmins. Better come away now, Mr. P. He looks like a young tiger."

Mrs. Plaskwith quitted the shop for the parlour. Her husband, putting his hands behind his back, and throwing back his chin, was about to follow her. Philip, who had remained for the last moment mute and white as stone, turned abruptly; and his grief taking rather the tone of rage than supplication, he threw himself before his master, and, laying his hand on his shoulder, said:

"I leave you--do not let it be with a curse. I conjure you, have mercy on me!"

Mr. Plaskwith stopped; and had Philip then taken but a milder tone, all
had been well.  But, accustomed from childhood to command--all his fierce
passions loose within him--despising the very man he thus implored--the
boy ruined his own cause.  Indignant at the silence of Mr. Plaskwith, and
too blinded by his emotions to see that in that silence there was
relenting, he suddenly shook the little man with a vehemence that almost
overset him, and cried:

"You, who demand for five years my bones and blood--my body and soul--a
slave to your vile trade--do you deny me bread for a mother's lips?"

Trembling with anger, and perhaps fear, Mr. Plaskwith extricated himself
from the gripe of Philip, and, hurrying from the shop, said, as he banged
the door:

"Beg my pardon for this to-night, or out you go to-morrow, neck and crop!
Zounds! a pretty pass the world's come to!  I don't believe a word about
your mother.  Baugh!"

Left alone, Philip remained for some moments struggling with his wrath
and agony.  He then seized his hat, which he had thrown off on entering--
pressed it over his brows--turned to quit the shop--when his eye fell
upon the till.  Plaskwith had left it open, and the gleam of the coin
struck his gaze--that deadly smile of the arch tempter.  Intellect,
reason, conscience--all, in that instant, were confusion and chaos.  He
cast a hurried glance round the solitary and darkening room--plunged his
hand into the drawer, clutched he knew not what--silver or gold, as it
came uppermost--and burst into a loud and bitter laugh.  The laugh itself
startled him--it did not sound like his own.  His face fell, and his
knees knocked together--his hair bristled--he felt as if the very fiend
had uttered that yell of joy over a fallen soul.

"No--no--no!" he muttered; "no, my mother,--not even for thee!" And, dashing the money to the ground, he fled, like a maniac, from the house.

At a later hour that same evening, Mr. Robert Beaufort returned from his country mansion to Berkeley Square.  He found his wife very uneasy and nervous about the non-appearance of their only son.  Arthur had sent home his groom and horses about seven o'clock, with a hurried scroll, written in pencil on a blank page torn from his pocket-book, and containing only these words,--

"Don't wait dinner for me--I may not be home for some hours.  I have met with a melancholy adventure.  You will approve what I have done when we meet."

This note a little perplexed Mr. Beaufort; but, as he was very hungry, he turned a deaf ear both to his wife's conjectures and his own surmises, till he had refreshed himself; and then he sent for the groom, and learned that, after the accident to the blind man, Mr. Arthur had been left at a hosier's in H----.  This seemed to him extremely mysterious; and, as hour after hour passed away, and still Arthur came not, he began to imbibe his wife's fears, which were now wound up almost to hysterics; and just at midnight he ordered his carriage, and taking with him the groom as a guide, set off to the suburban region.  Mrs. Beaufort had wished to accompany him; but the husband observing that young men would be young men, and that there might possibly be a lady in the case, Mrs. Beaufort, after a pause of thought, passively agreed that, all things considered, she had better remain at home.  No lady of proper decorum likes to run the risk of finding herself in a false position.  Mr. Beaufort accordingly set out alone.  Easy was the carriage--swift were the steeds--and luxuriously the wealthy man was whirled along.  Not a suspicion of the true cause of Arthur's detention crossed him; but he thought of the snares of London--or artful females in distress; "a melancholy adventure" generally implies love for the adventure, and money for the melancholy; and Arthur was young--generous--with a heart and a pocket equally open to imposition. Such scrapes, however, do not terrify a father when he is a man of the world, so much as they do an anxious mother; and, with more curiosity than alarm, Mr. Beaufort, after a short doze, found himself before the shop indicated.

Notwithstanding the lateness of the hour, the door to the private entrance was ajar,--a circumstance which seemed very suspicious to Mr. Beaufort. He pushed it open with caution and timidity--a candle placed upon a chair in the narrow passage threw a sickly light over the flight of stairs, till swallowed up by the deep shadow from the sharp angle made by the ascent. Robert Beaufort stood a moment in some doubt whether to call, to knock, to recede, or to advance, when a step was heard upon the stairs above--it came nearer and nearer--a figure emerged from the shadow of the last landing-place, and Mr. Beaufort, to his great joy, recognised his son.

Arthur did not, however, seem to perceive his father; and was about to pass him, when Mr. Beaufort laid his hand on his arm.

"What means all this, Arthur? What place are you in? How you have alarmed us!"

Arthur cast a look upon his father of sadness and reproach.

"Father," he said, in a tone that sounded stern--almost commanding--"I will show you where I have been; follow me--nay, I say, follow."

He turned, without another word re-ascended the stairs; and Mr. Beaufort, surprised and awed into mechanical obedience, did as his son desired. At the landing-place of the second floor, another long-wicked, neglected, ghastly candle emitted its cheerless ray. It gleamed through the open door of a small bedroom to the left, through which Beaufort perceived the forms of two women.  One (it was the kindly maidservant) was seated on a chair, and weeping bitterly; the other (it was a hireling nurse, in the first and last day of her attendance) was unpinning her dingy shawl before she lay down to take a nap.  She turned her vacant, listless face upon the two men, put on a doleful smile, and decently closed the door.

"Where are we, I say, Arthur?" repeated Mr. Beaufort.  Arthur took his father's hand-drew him into a room to the right--and taking up the candle, placed it on a small table beside a bell, and said, "Here, sir-- in the presence of Death!"

Mr. Beaufort cast a hurried and fearful glance on the still, wan, serene face beneath his eyes, and recognised in that glance the features of the neglected and the once adored Catherine.

"Yes--she, whom your brother so loved--the mother of his children--died in this squalid room, and far from her sons, in poverty, in sorrow! died of a broken heart!  Was that well, father?  Have you in this nothing to repent?"

Conscience-stricken and appalled, the worldly man sank down on a seat beside the bed, and covered his face with his hands.

"Ay," continued Arthur, almost bitterly--"ay, we, his nearest of kin--we, who have inherited his lands and gold--we have been thus heedless of the great legacy your brother bequeathed to us:--the things dearest to him-- the woman he loved--the children his death cast, nameless and branded, on the world.  Ay, weep, father: and while you weep, think of the future, of reparation.  I have sworn to that clay to befriend her sons; join you, who have all the power to fulfil the promise--join in that vow: and may Heaven not visit on us both the woes of this bed of death!"

"I did not know--I--I--" faltered Mr. Beaufort.

"But we should have known," interrupted Arthur, mournfully. "Ah, my dear father! do not harden your heart by false excuses. The dead still speaks to you, and commends to your care her children. My task here is done: O sir! yours is to come. I leave you alone with the dead."

So saying, the young man, whom the tragedy of the scene had worked into a passion and a dignity above his usual character, unwilling to trust himself farther to his emotions, turned abruptly from the room, fled rapidly down the stairs and left the house. As the carriage and liveries of his father met his eye, he groaned; for their evidences of comfort and wealth seemed a mockery to the deceased: he averted his face and walked on. Nor did he heed or even perceive a form that at that instant rushed by him--pale, haggard, breathless--towards the house which he had quitted, and the door of which he left open, as he had found it--open, as the physician had left it when hurrying, ten minutes before the arrival of Mr. Beaufort, from the spot where his skill was impotent. Wrapped in gloomy thought, alone, and on foot-at that dreary hour, and in that remote suburb--the heir of the Beauforts sought his splendid home. Anxious, fearful, hoping, the outcast orphan flew on to the death-room of his mother.

Mr. Beaufort, who had but imperfectly heard Arthur's parting accents, lost and bewildered by the strangeness of his situation, did not at first perceive that he was left alone. Surprised, and chilled by the sudden silence of the chamber, he rose, withdrew his hands from his face, and again he saw that countenance so mute and solemn. He cast his gaze round the dismal room for Arthur; he called his name--no answer came; a superstitious tremor seized upon him; his limbs shook; he sank once more on his seat, and closed his eyes: muttering, for the first time, perhaps, since his childhood, words of penitence and prayer. He was roused from this bitter self-abstraction by a deep groan. It seemed to come from the bed. Did his ears deceive him? Had the dead found a voice? He

started up in an agony of dread, and saw opposite to him the livid
countenance of Philip Morton: the Son of the Corpse had replaced the Son
of the Living Man!  The dim and solitary light fell upon that
countenance.  There, all the bloom and freshness natural to youth seemed
blasted!  There, on those wasted features, played all the terrible power
and glare of precocious passions,--rage, woe, scorn, despair.  Terrible
is it to see upon the face of a boy the storm and whirlwind that should
visit only the strong heart of man!

"She is dead!--dead! and in your presence!" shouted Philip, with his
wild eyes fixed upon the cowering uncle; "dead with--care, perhaps with
famine.  And you have come to look upon your work!"

"Indeed," said Beaufort, deprecatingly, "I have but just arrived: I did
not know she had been ill, or in want, upon my honour.  This is all a--a
--mistake: I--I--came in search of--of--another--"

"You did not, then, come to relieve her?" said Philip, very calmly.
"You had not learned her suffering and distress, and flown hither in the
hope that there was yet time to save her?  You did not do this?  Ha! ha!
--why did I think it?"

"Did any one call, gentlemen?" said a whining voice at the door; and the
nurse put in her head.

"Yes--yes--you may come in," said Beaufort, shaking with nameless and
cowardly apprehension; but Philip had flown to the door, and, gazing on
the nurse, said,

"She is a stranger! see, a stranger!  The son now has assumed his post.
Begone, woman!"  And he pushed her away, and drew the bolt across the
door.

And then there looked upon him, as there had looked upon his reluctant companion, calm and holy, the face of the peaceful corpse. He burst into tears, and fell on his knees so close to Beaufort that he touched him; he took up the heavy hand, and covered it with burning kisses.

"Mother! mother! do not leave me! wake, smile once more on your son! I would have brought you money, but I could not have asked for your blessing, then; mother, I ask it now!"

"If I had but known--if you had but written to me, my dear young gentleman--but my offers had been refused, and--"

"Offers of a hireling's pittance to her; to her for whom my father would have coined his heart's blood into gold! My father's wife!--his wife!-- offers--"

He rose suddenly, folded his arms, and facing Beaufort, with a fierce determined brow, said:

"Mark me, you hold the wealth that I was trained from my cradle to consider my heritage. I have worked with these hands for bread, and never complained, except to my own heart and soul. I never hated, and never cursed you--robber as you were--yes, robber! For, even were there no marriage save in the sight of God, neither my father, nor Nature, nor Heaven, meant that you should seize all, and that there should be nothing due to the claims of affection and blood. He was not the less my father, even if the Church spoke not on my side. Despoiler of the orphan, and derider of human love, you are not the less a robber though the law fences you round, and men call you honest! But I did not hate you for this. Now, in the presence of my dead mother--dead, far from both her sons--now I abhor and curse you. You may think yourself safe when you quit this room-safe, and from my hatred you may be so but do not deceive yourself. The curse of the widow and the orphan shall pursue--it shall cling to you and yours--it shall gnaw your heart in the midst of splendour--it shall cleave to the heritage of your son! There shall be a deathbed yet, beside which you shall see the spectre of her, now so calm, rising for retribution from the grave! These words--no, you never shall forget them--years hence they shall ring in your ears, and freeze the marrow of your bones! And now begone, my father's brother--begone from my mother's corpse to your luxurious home!"

He opened the door, and pointed to the stairs. Beaufort, without a word, turned from the room and departed. He heard the door closed and locked as he descended the stairs; but he did not hear the deep groans and vehement sobs in which the desolate orphan gave vent to the anguish which succeeded to the less sacred paroxysm of revenge and wrath.

### The Codes Of Hammurabi And Moses
### W. W. Davies

QTY

The discovery of the Hammurabi Code is one of the greatest achievements of archaeology, and is of paramount interest, not only to the student of the Bible, but also to all those interested in ancient history...

**Religion**      **ISBN:** *1-59462-338-4*      **Pages:132**

*MSRP $12.95*

### The Theory of Moral Sentiments
### Adam Smith

QTY

This work from 1749. contains original theories of conscience amd moral judgment and it is the foundation for systemof morals.

**Philosophy   ISBN:** *1-59462-777-0*      **Pages:536**

*MSRP $19.95*

### Jessica's First Prayer
### Hesba Stretton

QTY

In a screened and secluded corner of one of the many railway-bridges which span the streets of London there could be seen a few years ago, from five o'clock every morning until half past eight, a tidily set-out coffee-stall, consisting of a trestle and board, upon which stood two large tin cans, with a small fire of charcoal burning under each so as to keep the coffee boiling during the early hours of the morning when the work-people were thronging into the city on their way to their daily toil...

**Pages:84**

**Childrens    ISBN:** *1-59462-373-2*      *MSRP $9.95*

### My Life and Work
### Henry Ford

QTY

Henry Ford revolutionized the world with his implementation of mass production for the Model T automobile.  Gain valuable business insight into his life and work with his own auto-biography... "We have only started on our development of our country we have not as yet, with all our talk of wonderful progress, done more than scratch the surface. The progress has been wonderful enough but..."

**Pages:300**

**Biographies/      ISBN:** *1-59462-198-5*      *MSRP $21.95*

## The Art of Cross-Examination
## Francis Wellman

I presume it is the experience of every author, after his first book is published upon an important subject, to be almost overwhelmed with a wealth of ideas and illustrations which could readily have been included in his book, and which to his own mind, at least, seem to make a second edition inevitable. Such certainly was the case with me; and when the first edition had reached its sixth impression in five months, I rejoiced to learn that it seemed to my publishers that the book had met with a sufficiently favorable reception to justify a second and considerably enlarged edition. ..

**Reference**    **ISBN:** *1-59462-647-2*

**Pages:412**

*MSRP $19.95*

QTY

## On the Duty of Civil Disobedience
## Henry David Thoreau

Thoreau wrote his famous essay, On the Duty of Civil Disobedience, as a protest against an unjust but popular war and the immoral but popular institution of slave-owning. He did more than write—he declined to pay his taxes, and was hauled off to gaol in consequence. Who can say how much this refusal of his hastened the end of the war and of slavery ?

**Law**        **ISBN:** *1-59462-747-9*

**Pages:48**

*MSRP $7.45*

QTY

## Dream Psychology Psychoanalysis for Beginners
## Sigmund Freud

Sigmund Freud, born Sigismund Schlomo Freud (May 6, 1856 - September 23, 1939), was a Jewish-Austrian neurologist and psychiatrist who co-founded the psychoanalytic school of psychology. Freud is best known for his theories of the unconscious mind, especially involving the mechanism of repression; his redefinition of sexual desire as mobile and directed towards a wide variety of objects; and his therapeutic techniques, especially his understanding of transference in the therapeutic relationship and the presumed value of dreams as sources of insight into unconscious desires.

**Psychology**    **ISBN:** *1-59462-905-6*

**Pages:196**

*MSRP $15.45*

QTY

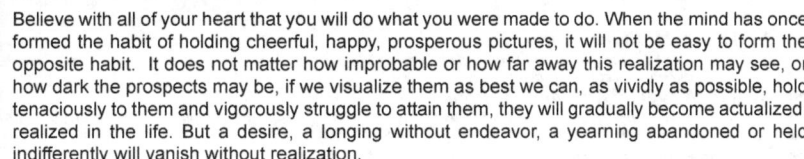

## The Miracle of Right Thought
## Orison Swett Marden

Believe with all of your heart that you will do what you were made to do. When the mind has once formed the habit of holding cheerful, happy, prosperous pictures, it will not be easy to form the opposite habit. It does not matter how improbable or how far away this realization may see, or how dark the prospects may be, if we visualize them as best we can, as vividly as possible, hold tenaciously to them and vigorously struggle to attain them, they will gradually become actualized, realized in the life. But a desire, a longing without endeavor, a yearning abandoned or held indifferently will vanish without realization.

**Self Help**      **ISBN:** *1-59462-644-8*

**Pages:360**

*MSRP $25.45*

QTY

QTY

**The Rosicrucian Cosmo-Conception Mystic Christianity** by *Max Heindel*  ISBN: *1-59462-188-8*  **$38.95**
*The Rosicrucian Cosmo-conception is not dogmatic, neither does it appeal to any other authority than the reason of the student. It is: not controversial, but is: sent forth in the, hope that it may help to clear...*  New Age/Religion Pages 646

**Abandonment To Divine Providence** by *Jean-Pierre de Caussade*  ISBN: *1-59462-228-0*  **$25.95**
*"The Rev. Jean Pierre de Caussade was one of the most remarkable spiritual writers of the Society of Jesus in France in the 18th Century. His death took place at Toulouse in 1751. His works have gone through many editions and have been republished...*  Inspirational/Religion Pages 400

**Mental Chemistry** by *Charles Haanel*  ISBN: *1-59462-192-6*  **$23.95**
*Mental Chemistry allows the change of material conditions by combining and appropriately utilizing the power of the mind. Much like applied chemistry creates something new and unique out of careful combinations of chemicals the mastery of mental chemistry...*  New Age Pages 354

**The Letters of Robert Browning and Elizabeth Barret Barrett 1845-1846 vol II**  ISBN: *1-59462-193-4*  **$35.95**
by *Robert Browning* and *Elizabeth Barrett*  Biographies Pages 596

**Gleanings In Genesis (volume I)** by *Arthur W. Pink*  ISBN: *1-59462-130-6*  **$27.45**
*Appropriately has Genesis been termed "the seed plot of the Bible" for in it we have, in germ form, almost all of the great doctrines which are afterwards fully developed in the books of Scripture which follow...*  Religion/Inspirational Pages 420

**The Master Key** by *L. W. de Laurence*  ISBN: *1-59462-001-6*  **$30.95**
*In no branch of human knowledge has there been a more lively increase of the spirit of research during the past few years than in the study of Psychology, Concentration and Mental Discipline. The requests for authentic lessons in Thought Control, Mental Discipline and...*  New Age/Business Pages 422

**The Lesser Key Of Solomon Goetia** by *L. W. de Laurence*  ISBN: *1-59462-092-X*  **$9.95**
*This translation of the first book of the "Lernegton" which is now for the first time made accessible to students of Talismanic Magic was done, after careful collation and edition, from numerous Ancient Manuscripts in Hebrew, Latin, and French...*  New Age/Occult Pages 92

**Rubaiyat Of Omar Khayyam** by *Edward Fitzgerald*  ISBN:*1-59462-332-5*  **$13.95**
*Edward Fitzgerald, whom the world has already learned, in spite of his own efforts to remain within the shadow of anonymity, to look upon as one of the rarest poets of the century, was born at Bredfield, in Suffolk, on the 31st of March, 1809. He was the third son of John Purcell...*  Music Pages 172

**Ancient Law** by *Henry Maine*  ISBN: *1-59462-128-4*  **$29.95**
*The chief object of the following pages is to indicate some of the earliest ideas of mankind, as they are reflected in Ancient Law, and to point out the relation of those ideas to modern thought.*  Religiom/History Pages 452

**Far-Away Stories** by *William J. Locke*  ISBN: *1-59462-129-2*  **$19.45**
*"Good wine needs no bush, but a collection of mixed vintages does. And this book is just such a collection. Some of the stories I do not want to remain buried for ever in the museum files of dead magazine-numbers an author's not unpardonable vanity..."*  Fiction Pages 272

**Life of David Crockett** by *David Crockett*  ISBN: *1-59462-250-7*  **$27.45**
*"Colonel David Crockett was one of the most remarkable men of the times in which he lived. Born in humble life, but gifted with a strong will, an indomitable courage, and unremitting perseverance...*  Biographies/New Age Pages 424

**Lip-Reading** by *Edward Nitchie*  ISBN: *1-59462-206-X*  **$25.95**
*Edward B. Nitchie, founder of the New York School for the Hard of Hearing, now the Nitchie School of Lip-Reading, Inc, wrote "LIP-READING Principles and Practice". The development and perfecting of this meritorious work on lip-reading was an undertaking...*  How-to Pages 400

**A Handbook of Suggestive Therapeutics, Applied Hypnotism, Psychic Science**  ISBN: *1-59462-214-0*  **$24.95**
by *Henry Munro*  Health/New Age/Health/Self-help Pages 376

**A Doll's House: and Two Other Plays** by *Henrik Ibsen*  ISBN: *1-59462-112-8*  **$19.95**
*Henrik Ibsen created this classic when in revolutionary 1848 Rome. Introducing some striking concepts in playwriting for the realist genre, this play has been studied the world over.*  Fiction/Classics/Plays 308

**The Light of Asia** by *sir Edwin Arnold*  ISBN: *1-59462-204-3*  **$13.95**
*In this poetic masterpiece, Edwin Arnold describes the life and teachings of Buddha. The man who was to become known as Buddha to the world was born as Prince Gautama of India but he rejected the worldly riches and abandoned the reigns of power when...*  Religion/History/Biographies Pages 170

**The Complete Works of Guy de Maupassant** by *Guy de Maupassant*  ISBN: *1-59462-157-8*  **$16.95**
*"For days and days, nights and nights, I had dreamed of that first kiss which was to consecrate our engagement, and I knew not on what spot I should put my lips..."*  Fiction/Classics Pages 240

**The Art of Cross-Examination** by *Francis L. Wellman*  ISBN: *1-59462-309-6*  **$26.95**
*Written by a renowned trial lawyer, Wellman imparts his experience and uses case studies to explain how to use psychology to extract desired information through questioning.*  How-to/Science/Reference Pages 408

**Answered or Unanswered?** by *Louisa Vaughan*  ISBN: *1-59462-248-5*  **$10.95**
*Miracles of Faith in China*  Religion Pages 112

**The Edinburgh Lectures on Mental Science (1909)** by *Thomas*  ISBN: *1-59462-008-3*  **$11.95**
*This book contains the substance of a course of lectures recently given by the writer in the Queen Street Hall, Edinburgh. Its purpose is to indicate the Natural Principles governing the relation between Mental Action and Material Conditions...*  New Age/Psychology Pages 148

**Ayesha** by *H. Rider Haggard*  ISBN: *1-59462-301-5*  **$24.95**
*Verily and indeed it is the unexpected that happens! Probably if there was one person upon the earth from whom the Editor of this, and of a certain previous history, did not expect to hear again...*  Classics Pages 380

**Ayala's Angel** by *Anthony Trollope*  ISBN: *1-59462-352-X*  **$29.95**
*The two girls were both pretty, but Lucy who was twenty-one who supposed to be simple and comparatively unattractive, whereas Ayala was credited, as her Bombwhat romantic name might show, with poetic charm and a taste for romance. Ayala when her father died was nineteen...*  Fiction Pages 484

**The American Commonwealth** by *James Bryce*  ISBN: *1-59462-286-8*  **$34.45**
*An interpretation of American democratic political theory. It examines political mechanics and society from the perspective of Scotsman James Bryce*  Politics Pages 572

**Stories of the Pilgrims** by *Margaret P. Pumphrey*  ISBN: *1-59462-116-0*  **$17.95**
*This book explores pilgrims religious oppression in England as well as their escape to Holland and eventual crossing to America on the Mayflower, and their early days in New England...*  History Pages 268

www.bookjungle.com *email: sales@bookjungle.com fax: 630-214-0564 mail: Book Jungle PO Box 2226 Champaign, IL 61825*

**QTY**

**The Fasting Cure** by *Sinclair Upton*                    ISBN: *1-59462-222-1*   **$13.95**   ☐
*In the Cosmopolitan Magazine for May, 1910, and in the Contemporary Review (London) for April, 1910, I published an article dealing with my experiences in fasting. I have written a great many magazine articles, but never one which attracted so much attention...* New Age/Self Help/Health Pages 164

**Hebrew Astrology** by *Sepharial*                    ISBN: *1-59462-308-2*   **$13.45**   ☐
*In these days of advanced thinking it is a matter of common observation that we have left many of the old landmarks behind and that we are now pressing forward to greater heights and to a wider horizon than that which represented the mind-content of our progenitors...* Astrology Pages 144

**Thought Vibration or The Law of Attraction in the Thought World**      ISBN: *1-59462-127-6*   **$12.95**   ☐
by *William Walker Atkinson*                                      Psychology/Religion Pages 144

**Optimism** by *Helen Keller*                    ISBN: *1-59462-108-X*   **$15.95**   ☐
*Helen Keller was blind, deaf, and mute since 19 months old, yet famously learned how to overcome these handicaps, communicate with the world, and spread her lectures promoting optimism. An inspiring read for everyone...* Biographies/Inspirational Pages 84

**Sara Crewe** by *Frances Burnett*                    ISBN: *1-59462-360-0*   **$9.45**   ☐
*In the first place, Miss Minchin lived in London. Her home was a large, dull, tall one, in a large, dull square, where all the houses were alike, and all the sparrows were alike, and where all the door-knockers made the same heavy sound...* Childrens/Classic Pages 88

**The Autobiography of Benjamin Franklin** by *Benjamin Franklin*      ISBN: *1-59462-135-7*   **$24.95**   ☐
*The Autobiography of Benjamin Franklin has probably been more extensively read than any other American historical work, and no other book of its kind has had such ups and downs of fortune. Franklin lived for many years in England, where he was agent...* Biographies/History Pages 332

| Name | |
| --- | --- |
| Email | |
| Telephone | |
| Address | |
| | |
| City, State ZIP | |

☐ **Credit Card**            ☐ **Check / Money Order**

| Credit Card Number | |
| --- | --- |
| Expiration Date | |
| Signature | |

*Please Mail to:   Book Jungle*
*PO Box 2226*
*Champaign, IL 61825*
*or Fax to:           630-214-0564*

## ORDERING INFORMATION

**web***: www.bookjungle.com*
**email***: sales@bookjungle.com*
**fax***: 630-214-0564*
**mail***: Book Jungle  PO Box 2226  Champaign, IL 61825*
**or PayPal** *to sales@bookjungle.com*

### *Please contact us for bulk discounts*

## DIRECT-ORDER TERMS

**20% Discount if You Order
Two or More Books**
Free Domestic Shipping!
Accepted: Master Card, Visa,
Discover, American Express

www.ingramcontent.com/pod-product-compliance
Lightning Source LLC
Chambersburg PA
CBHW080735250626
47170CB00010B/2838